It lay in the grass, tiny and white and burning. He stooped, put out his fingers. And then, in an instant, there was nothing. Nothing but darkness and oblivion. A split second demolition of the world of Richard Avery.

AND THEN—

"A series of questions has been prepared, to which it is hoped you will provide written answers. If you do, you will be rewarded . . . ."

AND THEN—

. . . one metal wall of his cell disappeared, revealing another exactly like his own. Except for one thing.

This one contained a woman.

AND THEN—

BY
EDMUND COOPER

TRANSIT

BY
EDMUND COOPER

A Division of Charter Communications Inc.
A GROSSET & DUNLAP COMPANY
1120 Avenue of the Americas
New York, New York 10036

TRANSIT

An ACE Book

Cover art by Dean Ellis

First Ace printing: March 1978

Printed in U.S.A.

We must love one another or die.
—W. H. Auden

ONE

THE FACE STARED back at Richard Avery, expressionless as a ghost. It was a bloodless face, he thought, the face of a man in limbo. It was the kind of face you did not look at too closely on the Underground in case its owner had died.

He moved away from the silvery grey mirror of the puddle and heard his feet squelch in the soggy earth. He gazed at the gaunt trees and the dull green emptiness of Kensington Gardens. London's Sunday traffic purred moodily in the distance; but February seemed determined to drown the landscape in a watery silence. And as the sad thin light of afternoon patiently died, it was possible to believe that Kensington Gardens was the most desolate place on earth.

The trouble with Avery was simple. He was recovering from influenza. The depression of the landscape and the depression of his state of mind matched perfectly, reinforcing each other. He should have stayed indoors watching the television, reading a book or playing his habitual meaningless games with the patterns on the wallpaper.

But, after a week's imprisonment in his two-roomed flat, after more than a hundred waking hours of solitary confinement with nothing but the memory of inadequacies and disappointments to keep him company, anything seemed preferable to the voices that never made a sound, the accusations that were never uttered.

At thirty-five, Richard Avery was a failure. Not an amateur failure; a professional failure. He had made a pretty good job of it. Fifteen years ago he had been all set to be an artist. Not necessarily a good painter, but at least one who slapped colour on the canvas as if he really meant it.

But that was fifteen years ago, when the world was young and he was very much in love. Her name was Christine. She had brown hair, brown eyes, a wide sensitive mouth and breasts that were compact, tantalizingly innocent and beautiful. She also had leukemia and a penchant for living gaily upon borrowed time. But the great thing about her was her tenderness. She loved Avery and she was sorry for him, deeply and tenderly sorry. For him, not for herself. That was the big joke. She knew that he needed tenderness. She knew that he needed all the tenderness he could get.

They lived together for just over a year; and during that time (in retrospect it seemed like an idyll at one with the great romances of history) he painted her more than a dozen times. He painted her naked, clothed, in repose, in landscapes and even in bed. He wanted to paint everything he knew about her, because there was so little time.

There was one thing he couldn't paint, though. He couldn't paint her tenderness. It was too big for a canvas, too brilliant for colour.

But it didn't last. It faded as her strength faded. And in the end, when she died, there was nothing left but disappointment and fear and the tight unspeakable loneliness of a small child. He was with her then, all the time. He watched the personality slowly dissolve in a sea of frustration and, ultimately, that small lovely body washed up like meaningless debris on the final shore.

Afterwards, he had a nervous breakdown. It was predictable. But when he came out of it, he couldn't hold a paintbrush without trembling, and he knew that he would never paint again. If he had been a great artist, nothing could have stopped him—not even the destruction of a hundred Christines. From which, of course, a conclusion could be drawn; and, to justify his failure, Avery quickly drew it.

The only problem that remained was to find a reasonably comfortable hole and crawl into it until time and mortality provided their own solution. The one thing he determined to avoid above all others was emotional involvement. His first experience would have to be his last. It was too painful ever to endure again. Not the ecstasy of loving, but the terrible dread of losing.

So he settled down to a visita of years without purpose, to a life of teaching art to children whose conception of the human form had been modified by cinema posters and deodorant advertisements, whose gods lived mysteriously in black discs, repeating parrot cries of anguish at the stimulus of a needle, and whose maturing values could be expressed in terms of pay checks, fast cars, drugged orgasms and the ultimate hypnosis of suburbia. He settled down to a life of pointless waiting, mere endurance, punctuated only by the recurring problem of evenings, week-ends, holidays and—occasionally—illness.

He did not live in the past. Neither did he live in the present or have any hope for the future. Regularly he contemplated suicide—and just as regularly failed to reach a decision.

Now, alone in Kensington Gardens with the late February afternoon closing round him like an expectant shroud, he began to hope that the edge of his depression would remain sharp long enough for him actually to do something about it.

But, regretfully, he knew that it wouldn't. He would merely carry the dull ache back to his two rooms and, as it were, vary the position slightly. Presently he would be well enough—or, at least, energetic enough—to become anaesthetized by another dose of teaching.

It was at that stage of introspection, as he turned in his tracks to walk back through the sodden half-freezing grass, that he noticed the crystal.

It lay in the grass, tiny and white and burning. At first he thought it was ice or a snow-flake. But neither ice nor snow are luminous; and this was so full of radiance that it seemed like a crystal of cold fire.

Suddenly, he knew it was the most beautiful thing in the world. He stooped, put out his fingers. And then, in an instant, there was nothing. Nothing but darkness and oblivion. A split second demolition of the world of Richard Avery.

TWO

AFTER A TIME—it might have been minutes or years—the oblivion somehow became less than absolute, and he knew he was dreaming. Images, half-formed, shimmered vaguely like reflections on a face of liquid darkness.

He saw stars. He literally saw stars. Whirlpools of stars—bright and blinding and frozen in the frothy glory of the great nebulae. He was drifting down a dark river of space. He was drifting to the end of the cosmos; and island universes—unimaginable dust bowls of light—seemed to flash by in the icy rapids of creation.

It was too cold—not physically cold, but spiritually cold. His half-conscious mind rejected the patterns of awful splendour, groping hungrily for meaning and relief and location. He came to a sun; and the sun had given birth to planets. One of the planets was blue and white with clouds, green with oceans, red and brown and yellow with islands.

'This,' said the voice, 'is home. This is the garden. This is the world where you will live and grow and know and understand. This is where you will discover enough but not too much. This is where life is. It is yours.'

The voice was gentle, but he was afraid of it. It came echoing at him down a draughty tunnel of centuries. Its whisper was thunder; and its words—such gentle words—were like the sentence for an unknowable crime.

He was afraid. Fear burned like acid through the fluffy twilight of consciousness. Suddenly, he was awake. Agonizingly awake. . . .

Avery found that he was lying on a bed. The bed was in a room whose walls were all metal. There were no windows. The ceiling glowed. It did not glow painfully but with enough light to provide pleasant illumination.

Obviously he was in hospital. He had passed out in Kensington Gardens, and they had taken him to hospital. But a hospital with metal walls. . . .

He sat up quickly, and was rewarded by a roaring in his ears, a throbbing behind his eyes. He waited patiently until his vision cleared, then tried to collect his thoughts.

He looked for the door.

There was no door.

He looked for a bell-push.

There was no bell-push.

He looked for escape.

There was no escape.

He was contained in a metal room like an animal in a trap. Someone must have put him there. But who?

Panic surged, and he fought it down. Panic surged again, and again he fought it down.

Perhaps he had had a nervous breakdown and this was some kind of asylum. Perhaps he only thought he was awake, but in reality he was still sleeping. Still dreaming a dream as inconsequential in its own way as the vision of cosmic creation.

He had an idea. It was absurd, but at least it was an idea. He pinched himself, and felt pain. He pinched himself harder, and felt more pain. Still he was not satisfied, for the possibility had occurred to him that he might easily experience the illusion of pain while dreaming.

Then he developed a line of thought that seemed to take care of both dream and reality. If he were still dreaming there could be no harm in exploring the situation—as far as exploration was possible. If he were not dreaming, then exploration was absolutely essential.

He got off the bed and looked around. There was a wash-stand. The design was peculiar, but pleasing. There was also a small half-boxed-in lavatory—at least, he supposed it was a lavatory—and a mirror.

In the centre of the room was a table and a dining chair. There was also an extremely light easy chair—so light that he found he could lift it with one hand. The floor was uncovered and appeared to be made of some kind of deep crimson plastic. It had a dull surface, restful to look at and pleasant to walk upon.

But the most interesting piece of furniture was the pedestal by the bed. On top of it lay a machine that looked something like a small and incredibly neat typewriter. The paper was already fed into it from an endless roll.

It was a typewriter with a difference, however. For even as he looked at it, it began to type. All by itself. There was hardly any noise and no visible movement, but the message was printed out on the roll of paper quickly and smoothly.

Avery gazed at it for a moment as if it might explode. Then he pulled himself together, sat down on the edge of the bed opposite the machine and began to read.

Do not be alarmed, said the message (he smiled cynically at that). *You are not in danger and you will be looked after with great care. Doubtless you have many questions to ask, but unfortunately there are some questions which cannot be answered. Whatever you need in order to live comfortably will be provided. Food and drink may be obtained on command. Your requests should be communicated by means of the keyboard.*

The machine stopped. Avery waited a few seconds, but that was all he was evidently going to get. He considered the message thoughtfully for a time, then put out two fingers—he had never been able to type with more than two fingers—and began to hit the keyboard.

He typed: *Where am I?*

His own message was not printed out on the paper roll, and he wondered if he had operated the machine properly. But as soon as he had finished, the reply was printed out for him.

No comment.

Avery stared at it and became angry. He punched out another question, hitting the keys as forcibly as he could.

Who are you?

Again the reply came immediately. *No comment.*

Why am I here?

No comment.

Avery spoke aloud for the first time. 'This is a bloody useful instrument, I must say!' The sound of his own voice shocked him. It was high, querulous. Whoever was on the other side of the metal wall must be enjoying himself—or themselves—

hugely. He determined to do what he could to minimize their satisfaction.

He began to tap out another question:

Why did the quick brown fox jump over the lazy dog?

Back came the reply:

Query: To which fox do you refer?

Avery smiled grimly. It was good to have the opposition asking questions. It made him feel that he had at least stolen a little of the initiative.

The one that jumped over the lazy dog, he tapped out.

Query: Which lazy dog?

The one that was jumped over by the quick brown fox.

There was a pause. Avery sat back, feeling idiotically pleased with himself. The pause lengthened. They—whoever they were—seemed: (a) to be taking the question seriously, and (b) seriously considering the possibility of an answer. All of which told him something. Not much, but something. They—the inscrutable they—didn't recognize a simple typewriting exercise. It was no great discovery, but at least it was information.

The reply came: *This question cannot be answered because insufficient data has been supplied. It is presumed that the answer, if any, does not have any immediate relationship to the subject's well-being.*

Avery felt that he had scored a moral victory. *They*—he visualized the word in italics—were either playing it dead-pan or else they were not very bright. He felt better.

The subject is depressed, he tapped. *The subject is imprisoned, frustrated, bewildered and bored. The subject is also hungry and thirsty. He pre-*

sumes that the bunch of raving maniacs with whom he is apparently dealing will at least have the decency to provide food and drink.

Query: In the present situation do you prefer water, an alcoholic drink, tea or coffee?

In the present situation, responded Avery, *I prefer an alcoholic drink–a large brandy–and coffee.*

There was no further communication. Avery sat and stared at his wristwatch. It was just over two minutes before anything happened. Then he became aware of a very faint scraping sound and looked up in time to see a rectangular panel slide back in the metal wall.

Behind it was a recess containing his meal. He got up and went to inspect. There was a plate of chicken salad—attractively laid out with crisp fresh lettuce, cress, beet-root and tomato—a knife, fork and spoon, and a miniature bottle of Martell Three Star. There was a pot of coffee, a tiny jug of cream, brown sugar, a coffee cup and saucer and a brandy glass. All of which was arranged upon a plastic tray.

He picked the tray up and took it to his table. The panel in the wall remained open.

Suddenly, he went to the typewriter that was not a typewriter and punched out another message.

You forgot the bread and butter.

Query: How many slices of bread?

One. White. Thin.

The wall panel closed. It opened again about ten seconds later.

There was a small plate on which lay the bread. One slice. White. Thin.

Avery sat down at the table and tackled his meal. The salad was delicious, the chicken sweet and tender. Evidently *they* did not intend that he should suffer from malnutrition.

As he ate, he tried to think clearly and sanely about his predicament. But his mind did not seem to be much in the mood for thought. It said, in effect, to him: There have been quite enough surprises for the time being. To hell with them! Something will sort itself out, sooner or later.

But would it? The predicament he was in was, itself, neither clear nor sane. One moment, it seemed to him, he was walking in Kensington Gardens; and the next moment he was waking up in what might well turn out to be a superior type of nut-house—or the inevitable mad millionaire's secret retreat in the Highlands.

He was more than confused: he was extremely doubtful about the nature of this particular frame of reality. The whole thing might easily be no more than a kind of dream within a dream—metal prison, inscrutable typewriter, chicken salad and all.

There was something worrying its way up into his conscious mind. Something about a crystal. . . . A glowing crystal. . . . Somewhere, somehow, he had seen a tiny crystal that glowed coldly with an intense point of frozen fire at its centre. But perhaps that, too, was part of the dream. . . .

He gave up the frail attempt at correlating thoughts and memories and deductions, and concentrated on the brandy and coffee. Something would sort itself out, sooner or later. It had to!

The brandy wasn't so great, but the coffee was quite good. Avery smacked his lips appreciatively. Then he knew there was something missing. Something vital. He wanted a cigarette.

He fished in his pockets and found his gas

lighter. But no cigarettes. Then he suddenly realized that somebody must have taken off his fleece-lined leather jacket. He looked round what he had already come to regard as his cell, but it was nowhere to be seen.

He went to the keyboard and tapped out: *Cigarettes, please.*

The response was immediate. *There is a supply in the trunk under your bed.*

Irrationally, Avery cursed himself for not having looked under the bed in the first place.

He hauled out the trunk. It was heavy and large and obviously new—the kind some travelling major or lower-echelon diplomat might buy for himself at the Army and Navy Stores. There were six heavy brass clips and a lock, but none of them were fastened. Avery lifted the lid back and peered inside. He was amazed.

There were several tropical shirts, three pairs of drill trousers and a couple of bush jackets—all new. There were two old pairs of leather sandals which he instantly recognized, and a couple of new pairs rather similar. There were vests and socks and a first-aid kit—all new.

His amazement became so great that it expired under its own weight. The whole thing was just too fantastic for words. He began to tip things out of the trunk untidily on to the floor as he delved deeper.

Together with his own toilet gear were some loaded razor-blade dispensers and about a dozen cakes of soap. Side by side with these was a small lightweight record player (mechanically operated as he discovered later) and a pile of new L.P. records. There were the Beethoven Fifths (symphony and piano concerto), the Bach Toccata and

Fugue and Double Violin concerto, some Strauss waltzes, selections from *My Fair Lady,* several Chopin pieces, the New World symphony and a recording of 'My Love is Like a Red, Red Rose' that held too many memories because it belonged to a special world—the one that he had shared briefly with Christine.

Avery stared at the collection helplessly. Somebody must have done a pretty good job of reading his mind, because each piece was a favourite. Each was assigned for a special mood or a special occasion in what used to be the neat and tidy life of Richard Avery.

He was momentarily frightened. Whoever knew this much about him already knew too much. His unseen captors already held a majority of aces.

But then he realized that his fear was not only futile, it was—for the time being, at least—inappropriate. Although he was a prisoner, so far the indications were that he was a privileged prisoner. He could only hope it was not simply a case of fattening up the goose. . . .

Some of the other things he came across surprised him even more. There was a tattered wallet in which he had kept a few photographs it seemed worth keeping—various shots of Christine, faded and rather formal shots of his parents, snaps of himself as a baby, child, youth and Second World War merchant seaman. There was a great quantity of tubes of oil paint, a palette, brushes and several canvas boards. There was a bundle of paper-backed novels, a couple of old diaries, about a ream of writing paper and a box of pencils.

And underneath everything were the cigarettes. Not just a packet. Not just a carton. But about five thousand. In fact the layer of packets—several deep—covered the entire bottom of the vast trunk. His favourite brand, needless to say!

Avery opened a packet, went back to his chair at the table, sat down and began to smoke in quick nervous puffs, surveying the debris by the bed.

Strewn about on the floor the contents of the trunk looked most incongruous. They gave the impression of either being impractical supplies for an absurd safari or the means by which a man might endure a stiffish prison sentence without going completely insane.

Avery poured himself a second cup of coffee, emptying the pot. As he sipped it he became aware of an intense weariness that seemed to crawl internally up his legs like some secret miniature alpinist, determined to reach the icy citadel of his brain.

Suddenly the cigarette tasted terrible, and he stubbed it out on his plate. He yawned and stood up, intending to put all the things back in the trunk just as he had found them—an exercise that at least might help to keep him awake.

He took two steps forward, yawned once more and realized that he was in no condition to start re-packing the trunk. The fatigue hit his brain with an almost physical impact. The room—the cell—began to ripple slightly. He knew that he would be very lucky if he managed to get as far as the bed.

He made it, but only just. Even as he slipped down the long tunnel of darkness he knew, oddly, that he had just remembered something important. But the memory and his awareness of it gently dissolved.

Avery was completely exhausted. Recent experience plus the after-effects of influenza had produced an overdraft of nervous energy that could only be reduced by sleep.

THREE

HE AWOKE WITH the feeling that he was not really waking at all, that he was merely re-entering a dream within a dream. But, he asked himself, what was the original dream? Answer: Kensington Gardens, London, teaching, the monotony of years without meaning. This dream at least was more vivid. It had an element of the absurd that was beginning to appeal to him.

He got up and inspected the cell. The remains of the meal had been cleared away, the contents of the trunk had been re-packed, and the trunk itself was back under his bed! There was one small change, however. His toilet things had been placed by the wash-stand. He decided there might be some virtue in freshening himself up.

Having used the lavatory with some relief and the oblique satisfaction of performing such simple animal functions, he stripped to the waist, gave himself a thorough wash in very hot water and shaved. After that, he felt ready for anything. More or less.

The packet of cigarettes he had opened was lying on the table. An ash-tray had been provided. He reached for the packet, took a cigarette, lit it and inhaled deeply. He began to think back.

But thinking back didn't seem to provide any useful information. He was at a loss. Eventually he seated himself beside the conversational typewriter, determined to get *something* out of it.

Question: *How long have I been here?*

Response: *No comment.*

Question: *Who the hell are you?*

Response: *No comment.*

Statement: *I think you are mad.*

Response: *No comment.*

Statement: *I don't really believe you exist.*

Response: *No comment. A series of questions has been prepared, to which it is hoped you will provide written answers. If you do, you will be rewarded.*

Statement: *To hell with your questions! I want a pot of tea. No food, just a pot of tea.*

Response: *It will be provided. Do you take sugar and milk?*

Statement: *Both.*

Avery began to pace about restlessly. The joke—if it was a joke—or the dream—if it was a dream—was getting just a shade too elaborate. He glanced at his watch, then he held it to his ear. It had stopped, of course. He felt totally disorientated. He might have been in the cell hours or days. He had no means of knowing.

He was about to ask what he knew was another 'no comment' question when the serving hatch opened. In the recess was a tray with a pot of tea, cup, saucer and spoon, milk and sugar. There was also a small sheaf of quarto sheets of paper and a pencil.

Avery took the tray to the table, sat down, poured himself a cup of tea and studied the papers. He snorted with disgust. He had seen papers like that before—hundreds of them. They contained fifty questions relating to number manipulation, spatial relationships, pattern recognition and verbal facility.

Suddenly, he was amused. It seemed poetic justice that, after so many years of inflicting them upon children, he should be faced with an intelligence test himself.

Do not agitate yourself, said the instructions at the top of the first sheet. *These questions are designed only to provide information. Your performance will not affect your future adversely or otherwise. Answer each question as quickly as possible. Do not return to any question you have failed to answer. Your co-operation will be appreciated.*

Do not agitate yourself! Avery laughed aloud. It sounded like some phrase from a foreign language smatter-book. Your co-operation will be appreciated! The devil it will, he thought cynically.

Then he remembered the bit about being rewarded, and wondered curiously what kind of reward *they* could possibly have in mind. The only worthwhile reward he could have would be freedom—but he was oddly sure that freedom was not even a remote possibility.

'Humour the bastards,' he told himself. 'Play it their way and see what happens. After all, there isn't much else to do.' He picked up the pencil.

Then he put it down again. First of all there was the small matter of providing himself with a time reference. He wound up his watch, set the fingers arbitrarily at twelve o'clock, silently declared the existence of midday on Day One (he had to begin somewhere) and at the same time resolved that he would create a time-sheet/calendar by making a mark on a piece of paper for every twelve hours that passed. There was writing paper in the trunk. As soon as he had finished the fool intelligence test that was what he would do. It might not be a bad idea if he kept a diary as well. Just in case he was in for a rather long stay.

Avery sighed and picked up the pencil once more. He looked at the first problem. Routine stuff. A number sequence. 5 8 12 17. He wrote down 23 in the space provided for the answer.

He did the first ten in about three minutes. Then he began to slow down.

Mingled with the increasing difficulty of the routine stuff were one or two that struck him as odd.

Sex is to Life as Fire is to: Furnace, Forest, Fluid, Fulfilment, Flame.

After some hesitation, he wrote: Furnace.

Then again, a little later.

Mountain is to Hill as Man is to: Ape, Woman, Child, Foetus.

He wrote: Ape.

And then, after half a dozen more conventional problems, another joker.

Power is to Wisdom as Religion is to: Devil, Hope, God, Salvation, Love.

God seemed to be the answer to that one.

There were several mathematical and pattern problems that Avery could not solve—or, at least, that he was not prepared to give the time and energy to solve—and he skipped them as instructed. Altogether, it took him a little over three-quarters of an hour to work through the questions. At the end of which he found that he had attempted to solve thirty-three of the problems—more or less satisfactory, he thought.

But the last one was the most intriguing of all. It was divided into three parts.

(a) *If you were the Supreme Being,* it said, *would you endow living things with infinite potential or would you set a limit upon their evolution?*

(b) *If you were the Supreme Being, do you think you would understand the meaning of death?*

(c) *If you were the Supreme Being, would you care more for the death of a virus or the birth of a galaxy?*

Avery wrote: (a) endow with infinite potential, (b), no, (c) the death of a virus.

And when he had put his pencil down, he came to the conclusion that the joke was very subtle. Very subtle indeed.

He lit another cigarette, then went to the talkative typewriter and punched out: *The monkey has earned its banana, gents. Test completed, IQ lamentable. I now claim the priceless reward.*

Back came the response: *Please return the test papers and tray to the recess.*

Suppose I don't?

You will be anaesthetized while they are collected. In that case it is recommended that you adopt a comfortable posture.

Goons! tapped Avery. He put the tea things back on the tray, childishly screwed the question papers into a tight ball and placed them in the recess. The panel closed.

Then he sat on the bed waiting for something to happen.

Nothing happened for about ten minutes.

Then suddenly, almost instantaneously, one metal wall of his cell disappeared, revealing another cell exactly like his own. Except for one thing.

This one contained a woman.

FOUR

SHE WAS BLONDE and in her mid-twenties. At least, thought Avery, she looked as if she *might* be in her mid-twenties; for she had the sort of vaguely attractive and subtly ageless face that might belong to a mature teenager or a youngish woman of forty.

She wore a red silk shirt and a pair of tight black slacks—and enough make-up for a party. Avery was sadly aware that the top two buttons of his shirt were undone—he only wore a tie when absolutely necessary—and his trousers displayed unmistakable signs of having been slept in.

All this passed through his mind—this ridiculous adding up of unimportant details—in the couple of seconds it took for the barrier of silence, surprise and immobility to crumble.

She was the first to move. She was the first to speak.

She came running towards him as if she were making a practiced entrance.

'Oh thank God! Thank God! I don't know who you are or why we're here. . . . But at least you're human. I was beginning to think I might never see another human face again.'

Her voice was pleasant, her delivery was excellent. And when she had finished, she burst into tears. Before he really knew what was happening, Avery found that he had put his arms around her and that she was clinging to him tightly.

This, too, was so improbable that it could easily be part of a dream.

'Take it easy,' he heard himself murmuring. 'Take it easy.' Then, idiotically: 'Neither of us are dead yet.'

She broke away. 'Hell, I'm ruining my make-up. . . . What's your name?'

'Richard Avery. What's yours?'

She smiled archly: 'Don't you ever watch TV? No, that's stupid. You can't watch TV here, of course.'

Recognition dawned. 'I used to watch quite a lot. The only thing I ever conscientiously tried to avoid was that endless hospital series. You're Barbara Miles, of course.'

'In the flesh,' she said.

Avery smiled. 'Not necessarily. I have a theory I may be dreaming.'

'The nightmare is mutual,' she retorted. 'What in heaven's name is it all about?'

'Damned if I know. Have you any idea how you got here?'

She shook her head. 'The last thing I remember was this wretched diamond. I thought it might have fallen out of somebody's ring—though goodness knows it looked too big for that. I rememeber bending down to pick it up. Then lights out.'

The information gave Avery a jolt. He remembered about the crystal instantly, and saw it once more in his mind's eye—cold and lustrous and blinding.

'Well, say something,' she said nervously. 'I didn't make it all up.'

Avery looked at her and noticed the lines of tension at the corners of her eyes. The nightmare was decidedly mutual.

'This diamond,' he said, 'it wouldn't have been in Kensington Gardens by any chance?'

She stared at him. 'Hyde Park, as it happens—but how would *you* know?'

'The dividing line between Hyde Park and Kensington Gardens is more or less imaginary,' he said without humour. 'Mine was in Kensington Gardens. Not a diamond—at least, I think not. Just a crystal.'

There was a pause while each of them considered possibilities—and got nowhere.

'I need a cigarette,' she said at length.

He gave her one and then took one himself.

She inhaled deeply. 'What did you say your name was? It just shows what a state I'm in. Can't even remember a name.'

'Richard Avery.'

She laughed shrilly. 'Pleased to meet you, Richard. And welcome to the club.'

'I'm more than glad to meet you,' he retorted with conviction. 'I was rather afraid the membership was restricted to one.'

'Say my name,' she said. 'Please.'

'Barbara.'

'Say it again.'

'Barbara.'

She sighed. 'It doesn't sound too bad. . . . I'm sorry. You must think I'm going round the bend. I probably am. For a while—in fact until that wall disappeared—I was beginning to think I might not be me. . . . Sorry again. That doesn't make much sense, does it?''

'It makes a lot of sense.'

'In fact,' confided Barbara,'I wasn't really sure I was me until I saw you. Then for some damn silly reason there didn't seem to be any doubt about it.'

A thought suddenly struck Avery. 'Before we start nursing each other—no, I don't mean that nastily—we'd better pool our information, such as it is. God knows how long it will be before the Goons put the wall back or get up to some other dodge. We may have another ten minutes or we may have all day—I mean several hours, anyway. So let's make the most of it.'

'Nothing to report, sergeant,' said Barbara. 'Except that I feel a bit better.'

'Have you seen anything of them?'

'Who, the mad scientists?'

'Is that *your* theory?'

'It's as good as any. . . . No I haven't seen a damn thing. . . . To tell the truth,' she added hesitantly, 'I had an idea they might be watching. I got so neurotic and bored that I took all my clothes off and lay down in the classical position for rape.' She giggled. 'Nothing happened. Either they weren't watching or they weren't interested—or both. . . . I'm beginning to think I really may be going round the bend after all.'

Avery pushed the disturbingly vivid picture to the back of his mind. 'Have you any idea how long you have been here?' he asked.

'That's an easy one,' said Barbara. She glanced at her watch. 'Not quite forty-eight hours. I'm keeping a careful tally—just in case I begin to think it's years.'

'Did you have anything with you when you woke up—I mean personal possessions.'

'No. But I found a whole heap of stuff in a trunk under the bed. I don't know how they managed to get hold of it, because I share—correction, shared—a flat with three other girls.'

'You communicate by that teletype thing, I suppose.'

'Four-letter words now,' said Barbara. 'I'm trying to find out what happens if I'm not ladylike. . . . Incidentally, they had me doing a stack of fool questions. Said I'd be rewarded.' She grinned. 'I suppose you are the reward.'

'So far,' said Avery, 'our experiences are pretty identical. Except that I didn't manage to keep a time check.'

'Then what have we learned?'

He shrugged. 'Nothing much. Except that we aren't alone.'

'But when you come to think of it,' said Barbara seriously, 'that's a pretty big something.'

At that moment Avery's typewriter started typing. He and Barbara peered at the message.

In ten minutes it will be necessary for you to occupy your separate rooms.

'Hell!' exploded Barbara. 'Hell and damnation!'

Avery typed back: *We wish to remain together.*

The response came immediately. *You will not be separated for long, providing you each answer the next series of questions as accurately as possible.*

We do not wish to be separated at all, and neither do we wish to answer any more questions.

No comment. You have nine minutes left.

'Here,' said Barbara, 'let me tell 'em.' She typed: *Get knotted.*

Avery was amused. He was beginning to like Barbara. She had quite a personality. He wondered if the machine would print out a reply, but it maintained a dignified silence.

'So,' said Barbara angrily, 'the mad scientists

are feeling playful again.'

Avery gave her a thin smile. 'The question is: do we behave like obedient dogs or do we provoke them?'

'Don't call me a dog, please. I'm just a common or garden bitch. . . . Dammit, you're the man. You'll have to decide. That's what men are for—and other things.'

'You don't want to be emancipated about it?'

'I don't want to be emancipated about anything,' she replied firmly. 'I can usually get what I want without resorting to equal votes.'

Avery thought for a moment. 'Then we'll play it the hard way,' he decided, 'and see what happens. Meanwhile, let's put our heads together and see if we can't come up with a lead.'

'They are probably listening,' she warned.

'I'm sure they are. I think it's all part of the treatment—especially bringing us together.'

For a while, they talked round the problem; but since they had so little to go on, there was precious little that could be deduced. So far, neither of them had suffered physically—apart from being 'anaesthetized'—and it seemed reasonable to assume that their captors did not intend to use more violence than was strictly necessary for whatever purpose *they* had in mind.

But what that purpose was—well, that was the big question. In desperation, Avery and Barbara tried random suggestions. Bearing in mind how little they actually knew, it seemed as good a way as any of trying to hit on the truth.

Barbara suggested plain, good, old-fashioned kidnapping. But Avery pointed out that conventional kidnappers did not usually ply their victims with intelligence tests. Besides, the resources of the prison seemed rather beyond either the ability or the imagination of the normally abnormal criminal mind. Added to which, the contents of both trunks indicated that they were in for quite a long stay—and not all of it would be spent in prison, evidently.

The mad-scientist notion also was dismissed. Apart from any other considerations, it was too trite, too wildly implausible. However, Barbara wanted to stick to the idea of madness at least, because it seemed to be an essential ingredient of the whole operation; but Avery was not so sure.

'So far the purpose and the technique are pretty well outside our terms of reference,' he said. 'I don't think we can apply any conventional criteria.'

'Stop talking like something that just crawled out of Cambridge,' said Barbara drily. 'All you mean is that we haven't got a single clue.'

'No, I mean just the opposite. I have a feeling that the clue lies in the incomprehensibility of the whole thing. It's as if the mind or minds behind this business just don't operate on our level. There's an alien factor, an *otherness* about all that's happened to us.'

Suddenly, the typewriter woke up again. *Please return to your separate accommodation.*

'Now for the fireworks,' said Barbara. She sat down and typed back. *No thank you. We just got married.*

The machine was not amused. *It is necessary for you to answer further questions,* it sent back primly. *Your cooperation will be appreciated.*

Barbara was about to punch out a further message of defiance, but Avery said: 'Let it play by itself. I think the general idea has got across.'

Barbara sighed. 'You're the captain. But I like being childish. It improves my morale.'

There was a few seconds of silence, during which they both gazed about them apprehensively as if retaliation might leap out at them from the walls or from the illuminated ceiling. But nothing happened, and they were left with a feeling of anticlimax.

'It looks as if they're thinking it over,' suggested Avery. 'Normally they seem to respond pretty quickly.'

'Maybe they haven't had a case like this before.' Barbara sounded more flippant than she felt.

'Well, let's try to forget about them for a bit, otherwise the waiting will get on our nerves. . . . Now where was I?'

'Otherness—that's where you were.'

'Yes,' he said, 'otherness is the right word, I think. . . .We don't belong, the situation doesn't belong—it's unreal, somehow not properly human.'

'Inhuman?'

'Perhaps, but not in the ordinary sense. Non-human is better. For example, I wouldn't be at all surprised if we were using that thing,' he gestured to the teletypewriter, 'to communicate with a computer. And a not very flexible computer at that.'

'I have an odd conviction that it wasn't a computer that snatched me out of Hyde Park,' objected Barbara.

'Maybe, but—' Avery got no further.

At that moment the wall panel slid back. Instinctively, they both looked to see what the recess contained. Their attention was immediately drawn to one tiny object.

It was a crystal, flawless and beautiful, brilliant and blinding. It was a crystal of pure light containing the mystery of absolute darkness.

FIVE

HE WAS INVISIBLE. He was no more than a wisp of thought and feeling in the empty garden of creation. He was a rustle of wind through the alleyways of time, a moment of sadness in the long tremendous joy of unbeing. He was nothing and everything. He was alone.

Yet not alone.

Christine swam towards him through the stars. And the stars became the leaves of autumn, brown and gold, whipped to dancing on the crest of unheard music. And a whole lost world throbbed back into existence—a world that was young and green with living.

Christine whispered: 'Wherever you are, whatever you do, my dear one, I am part of it. For what is between us is above time and place and life and death. . . . There is a journey to be made, my darling. Make it. There is a dream to be dreamt, a faith to be kept, a challenge to be taken. Our love is part of the dream, the faith, the challenge. Make of it something new. Make it bright and glorious. Give it freedom.'

He wanted to speak: but an invisible eye, a wisp of thought, a rustle of wind has no voice. He wanted to say: 'Christine! Christine! You and you only. Nothing else. Not living or loving, not journeying or creating. But you and you only. . . . '

That is what he wanted to say; but there were no words. They would not form in the darkness. They would not pass through the black backcloth between desiring and knowing.

Christine dissolved, and there was emptiness only.

But the emptiness filled with the great green eye of a planet. It stared at him. It stared like a woman who knows she is fair. It stared like an animal waiting to conquer or be tamed.

'This,' said the voice, 'is home. This is the garden. This is the world where you will live and grow and understand. This is where you will discover enough but not too much. This is where life is. It is yours.'

He had heard the voice before. He had heard the words before. But he did not understand the message.

He was afraid. Afraid because he did not understand. Afraid because he knew there was too much and too little to understand. Afraid because he was alone, and the loneliness was deeper than pain. . .

Avery woke. There was sweat on his forehead.

He was lying neatly—too neatly—on the bed, arms by his side, like a patient coming out of anaesthetic. He remembered the last time, and sat up slowly. The throbbing in his head was not too bad.

He looked round. Barbara had disappeared, the wall had returned and he was once more in solitary confinement. He smiled weakly, thinking of the thoughts that Barbara would be thinking, the words she would doubtless be arranging in attractively unladylike profanities.

The panel was still open, but there was no crystal in the recess. Only a single sheet of paper. And a pencil.

'So much for passive resistance,' thought Avery. He ought to have realized that the crystal would be used. It was just too easy.

He took the pencil and paper to his table, sat down and looked at the questions. No intelligence test this time. Something rather more personal. Fortunately, it was mostly yes-or-no stuff. And there wasn't much of it.

Do you believe in God, as a person whose ethic may be interpreted by men? He wrote: No.

Do you believe that the end justifies the means? He wrote: Sometimes it does: sometimes it doesn't.

Do you desire immortality? He wrote: No.

Do you think you are courageous, more than normally courageous or a coward? He wrote: A coward.

Does your present situation cause stress? He wrote: Don't be stupid.

Would you be willing to die for an ideal? He wrote: I don't know.

Do you think that men are superior to animals? He wrote: Only in some things.

Are you sexually potent? He wrote: I believe so.

What do you fear most? He wrote: Insanity.

Do you think that warfare can be justified? He wrote: Sometimes.

Have you ever committed murder? That, thought Avery, was a peach of a question. He wrote: I don't think so.

Have you ever killed anyone? The imagined faces of three nameless airmen loomed sharply and briefly in his consciousness. He wrote: Yes.

Whom, if anyone, do you love? Feeling like a traitor, Avery wrote: Myself.

That was the lot. He glanced through his answers then returned the paper to the recess. Presently the panel closed.

He went to the inscrutable typewriter and tapped out: *Now will you move that blasted wall again?*

Back came the answer: *Very soon. Please be patient.*

Avery lit a cigarette and began to pace up and down. The situation was getting more and more fantastic. The most annoying thing seemed to be that he was completely robbed of initiative. *They* were having it all their own way; and that he resented bitterly.

Back once more to the question of who they were: answer—there was no answer. . . . But there had to be! And Avery was acutely aware of the mental barrier separating rational thought from irrational conviction. To hell with rational thought, he told himself irritably. Rational thought was no good for a situation like this. Only the irrational would do—and probably even that wasn't good enough.

Out with it then! Out with the bloody stupid conviction that has been building up at the back of your mind like water behind a dam.

Avery took a deep breath and said it aloud. 'They're not human beings at all. They are bloody bug-eyed monsters.'

The words exploded in the quietness of the room, seemed to echo thunderously from the metal walls.

And at that moment, as if at a signal, the wall that had separated him from Barbara disappeared.

Only this time it was not Barbara on the other side. It was someone else.

A girl. Brown hair, wide frightened eyes, body subtly mature, face round and young.

'Where's Barbara? Who are *you?*' snapped Avery. His voice sounded harsh. He didn't mean it to be, but it was.

'I'm Mary Durward. . . . I—I. . . . How did you get there?' She was clearly very frightened.

Avery remembered that he was unwashed, unshaved. He smiled. He must be looking rather sordid, like something sinister out of a B feature. Hell, this *was* a B feature. 'There was a girl called Barbara Miles in the cell next to mine,' he explained. 'At least, I thought there was. You can't be sure of any damn thing in this place. . . . My name is Richard Avery, by the way.'

She brightened a little when she saw that he was not as fierce as he had looked. 'The same thing has happened to me. The man next door was called Tom Sutton. They—they let us talk together. Then there were some more questions to answer, and we were separated again.'

Avery thought for a moment. 'Let's try to piece a bit more of the jigsaw together. Where did they collect you—Kensington Gardens or Hyde Park?'

She looked startled. 'Kensington Gardens. How did you know?'

'I've made a study of the habits of Abducted Persons,' he said drily. 'There was an attractive little crystal, I suppose.'

'I thought it was somebody's brooch,' she admitted. 'And I—'

'And you bent down to pick it up. The next thing you know, you're in the nut-house. Right?'

She smiled. There was something very pleasing

about her smile. Suddenly, Avery was intensely sorry for her. She didn't look anywhere near as tough or resilient as Barbara. She only looked about eighteen. And lost. Very lost.

'Do you know what it's all about?' she asked hopefully.

'No. I'm afraid I don't know anything at all—except that it seems to be a real situation. At first I thought it was all in my overwrought little mind. . . . May I step into your parlour, said the spider to the fly.'

She smiled again. Avery offered her a cigarette and took one himself. They sat down together on the edge of her bed like—as he thought—a couple of stranded tourists waiting for a train that they knew will never arrive.

'Let's start at the beginning,' he said, 'and see if we can't find some common denominator. Where do you live, how old are you, what do you do?'

'Lancaster Gate,' she answered. 'Twenty three, secretary.'

'Married?'

'No.'

'Do you live with anyone?'

She shook her head.

'What about the man next door—I mean the man that was in the next cell to you?'

'Tom Sutton. He was picked up in Kensington Gardens, too. He's a public relations type. Quite nice, but still—'

'Still a type?'

'Perhaps I'm being unfair. . . . He seems to think the whole thing could be some weird kind of publicity gimmick.'

Avery shrugged. 'Tell me that long enough, and

I'll believe it myself. . . . Do you know if he is married?'

'I'm not sure, but I don't think so.'

'Barbara doesn't have the married look, either,' said Avery. 'Anyway, let's make assumptions just for the hell of it. Now what have we got so far? One TV actress, one secretary, one P.R. man and one teacher—that's me, by the way—all blessedly single and with dangerous tendencies to stroll in the park and spot magic crystals. . . . It's not really very statistical.'

'What do you mean?'

'If it was just random selection, somebody ought to have been married.' He sighed. 'I don't know. Maybe Barbara or Tom is.'

'Would that make any difference?'

'It might. I'm just grasping at straws. . . . A personal question: are you in love with anybody?'

She shook her head emphatically. 'I was once.'

'So was I. Still am, I suppose, but she's dead. . . . I don't think Barbara is in love particularly. What about this Tom Sutton?'

'I don't know.'

'Then make an intelligent guess.'

'I should say not, but I don't really know.'

'That will have to do. Anyway, it fits a theory.' He laughed. 'I don't mind twisting the odd facts to fit a theory.'

'What is the theory?'

Avery was silent for a moment or two. Then he said: 'Well, I'll stick my neck out. I don't think it happened by accident. I think we were all chosen. If my theory fits, we were chosen because we didn't have any strong emotional ties. Now why were we chosen? Answer: to undergo some sort of test. So far, *they*—whoever *they* might be—have taken pretty good care of us, but they have also been finding out a devil of a lot about us: the way we think, how bright we are, what our emotional attitudes are. Now comes the gilt-edged question: who or what are *they?* And inevitably we get the bumper fun book answer: *they* are not human. They are not human because they didn't use what may be loosely called human techniques to set up this little experiment. That thing,' he gestured towards Mary's teletypewriter, is the sort of mechanism that would be used by some non-human being to establish contact without giving us all fits. And while this cell itself could probably be very easily constructed by present-day technology, its not the sort of thing that would be. . . . Now, how does all that sound?'

Mary shivered. 'It sounds horrible—and plausible.'

'I bet you've got quite a stack of supplies in that trunk under your bed, haven't you?'

She nodded.

He smiled grimly. 'There's every sign that it's going to be quite a long experiment—phase two to be conducted elsewhere.'

Mary offered no comment. Avery was about to develop his ideas further when he became aware of a faint scraping sound.

'Look at the floor!' he commanded urgently, and did so himself.

'What's happening?' she asked, bewildered.

'I just heard the panel open—your panel, I think. Maybe there's a crystal in the recess. That's how Barbara and I were caught last time. We ignored instructions and got knocked cold.'

'We're going to have to look up sooner or later.

We can't stay like this. Besides, we haven't done anything wrong, have we?'

'Who the devil knows what's right or wrong in this place?' he demanded irritably. 'Wait a minute. Only one of us will look—and I've just elected myself on a seniority basis. If I keel over, don't do anything. Keep your gaze well away from the hatch. We'll make them think of something else. All right? I'm going to look now.'

There was a pause, then Avery said disgustedly: 'Serves me right. You can relax, Mary. It's coffee for two.'

She looked up and giggled. 'I forgot to tell you. I ordered coffee just before the wall slid back.'

'For two?'

'No. I didn't think there would be company.'

'Then we must have an intelligent waitress,' he said drily.

The coffee relaxed them, transforming the tension into an almost social atmosphere. They smoked a couple of cigarettes and, for the time being, Avery decided not to develop his bug-eyed monster theory any further. Mary Durward looked very much like a girl in need of some reassurance. The trouble was he didn't know what kind of reassurance it was possible to give.

Playing it safe he decided to concentrate on finding out a bit more about her personal background. Apart from the fact that he was naturally interested in her, it was just possible that she might provide information that would be of use in building up theories—even though it was highly probable that any theories built up on the present fund of evidence would eventually collapse like a house of cards.

But conversation for its own sake was something. In fact, it was a hell of a lot—the kind of therapy they could both use in liberal doses.

He learned that Mary worked in the West End office of Empire Chemicals, that she had been with the company five years, that her boss was called Mr. Jenkins (he was mildly surprised that anybody could still be called Mr. Jenkins), that she played tennis and Scrabble and liked Dixieland jazz, that her parents were dead and that her fiancé had disconcertingly married someone else.

In return he told her a little about himself. Presently he was even telling her about Christine. Which was surprising, because he never told anyone about Christine. Not unless he was drunk or knew the listener very well. In this case, neither circumstance obtained. But, he told himself with amusement, this was quite an exceptional case, really: it was the first time he had ever been imprisoned by bug-eyed monsters. He didn't regard them (and it had to be plural for there was surely too much for one to handle) as bug-eyed monsters in the literal sense. Well, not necessarily. More in the metaphorical sense. And that was possibly even more disturbing.

'You're miles away,' said Mary. 'What were you thinking about?'

'About how I would like to be miles away,' he answered lightly. 'Or at least, back in Kensington Gardens with the prospect of returning to my empty little flat. I never knew it could be so attractive.'

'I do and I don't,' she remarked inscrutably.

'Do and don't what?'

'Want to get away from here. I mean I do, of course, really—but not until I've found out what it's all about.'

Avery was surprised. The girl had more spirit than he would have thought. He was about to predict that *they* would not let their victims find anything out if it could possibly be avoided, when Mary's teletypewriter began to chatter away.

Please return to your own accommodation, it said. *You will not be separated for long.*

'That's what the wretched machine told us last time,' said Avery moodily. 'But it wasn't exactly telling the truth, was it?'

'You never know,' said Mary, 'we might find later that it was. . . . It seems to have been pretty honest about most things.'

Avery laughed. 'No comment. That's the catch-phrase in our crazy little world. What I mean is that it put *us* together instead of me and Barbara and you and Tom.'

'I think it's probably making introductions,' she said seriously. 'Did you want to see Barbara again very much?'

'Yes, of course. But not in a special personal sense. What about Tom?'

She shrugged. 'Not particularly. He was rather tiring.'

'Am I rather tiring?'

'Not in the way that Tom was.'

Avery was amused. At least he seemed to have a negative virtue.

The teletypewriter chattered at them once more. *It is necessary for you to return to your own accommodation immediately,* it said, adding emphasis to the original message. *Please then lie down on your own bed and await further developments.*

Mary giggled. 'That seems to indicate breathtaking possibilities.'

Avery smiled. 'Not with these goons, it doesn't—well, not like that. I shouldn't be at all surprised if it is some kind of remote-controlled medical check. They are very inquisitive little beasties. . . . I suppose I'd better get back to my own state room, otherwise it will be crystals for two.'

They both lay down on their beds, waiting—and feeling oddly embarrassed.

'It was nice meeting you,' called Mary.

'A pleasure,' he answered. 'Let's hope it's a tea-party for four next time. We might be able to work something out if we could all get together.'

The wall came back. It came back with a speed that astonished Avery. But then he had other things to think about than the kind of mechanism that could project walls almost instantaneously; for the illuminated ceiling began to darken slowly. And presently he was lost in a roomful of blackness.

But for a moment only.

Where the ceiling had been there was now a magnificent window—a window on the universe.

They were stars.

Stars in their millions.

Lights that spattered the sky.

That it was real, Avery did not doubt. Nothing but reality could provide the sheer brilliance, the hard unwinking intensity, the awful remoteness of so many living suns. They hung motionless, infinitely small and great beyond imagining. They hung like lanterns on the far Christmas tree of creation. They hung like teardrops of frozen fire.

For a moment, the impact was so great that Avery wanted to curl up like a foetus, to reject the outward reality and know only the blank, bleak security of his square metallic womb. But the moment passed; and he was hypnotized into acceptance.

He never knew there could be so many stars. He had known intellectually, of course, that the universe contained stars outnumbering the grains of sand on the shores of the world's oceans. But he had never known that this was real, that it was anything more than empty words.

But now the knowledge etched itself into his brain, swallowed his personality, shrank his ego to a single molecule of humility, seared all his human experience into a lonely atom of wonder.

There, above or below—for he no longer knew whether he was looking up or down—were blank spaceways curling over the deserts of infinity. There, above and below and beyond, were the milky golden nebulae of star cities—impossible flowers of fire and time locked in the dark glass of the cosmos. There, if anywhere, was the face of God.

He wanted to die, he wanted to laugh, he wanted to sing or cry out with pain and fear. He wanted to dance for joy and simultaneously mourn the absolute tragedy.

He did nothing. He could do nothing. Nothing except stare with a subtle anguish that came near to praying.

Then suddenly the universe began to dance. It swung slowly into the gay leap of a long parabola. Stars and star cities, space, time and creation swung slowly round the fixed microcosm that was Richard Avery.

And then there was the greatest shock of all.

The planet danced into being. *The* planet. A pumpkin filled with light. A celestial pumpkin whose face was green with oceans, blue and white with clouds, red and brown and yellow with islands.

It was entirely beautiful. It was a ball of life.

There was a remembered voice. A voice remembered over centuries and light-years and the long limbos of dreams and imagination.

'This,' said the voice, 'is home. This is the garden. This is the world where you will live and grow and understand. This is where you will discover enough but not too much. This is where life is. It is yours.'

Richard Avery's eyes were filled with tears, because the pain and the knowledge and the promise and the truth were unbearable. His body was icy cold because, also, there was fear.

He knew he could not take any more. And at the moment of knowing, a tiny crystal burned into transient glory above the face of the planet.

It was a crystal he already recognized.

It was the crystal of oblivion.

It was an act of mercy.

SIX

AVERY OPENED HIS EYES. The sky was blue—an intense, lovely blue—the kind of blue that nobody could ever paint. He lay staring at it for a moment or two, staring and listening to the sound of the sea. And thinking back. . . .

He had been in a kind of prison, and the roof of the prison had dissolved into a window on the universe, and then it was as if God had spoken. And the whole sequence was just too damned fantastic for words.

So now he was lying on a camp bed on the sea-shore, listening to the waves and drinking in the warmth of the early morning sun. It was a pleasant hallucination. He hoped this one would stay with him for a while.

'Ah, you're awake at last!'

Avery turned his head cautiously, then sat up. The hallucination contained a man sitting on another camp bed and smoking a cigarette. It also contained two more beds bearing the presumably sleeping forms of Barbara and Mary. It also contained an infinity of ocean, a superb beach, a fringe of what looked vaguely like palm trees and a litter of camping equipment that might have been left over from a boy scouts' jamboree.

'I'm Tom Sutton. I imagine you are Richard Avery. . . . Quite an interesting situation, don't you think?'

'Quite,' said Avery. He took the outstretched hand. 'Pleased to meet you.' It sounded ridiculous, even though it happened to be true.

Tom Sutton was a tall, solidly built character, and looked as if he could give Avery a couple of stone without missing it. Although he only seemed about thirty, his stomach tended to bulge slightly with its tell-tale evidence of good living.

'The girls are still out,' said Tom. 'That Mickey-Finn-type crystal certainly packs a wallop.' He sighed. 'Wish I'd had the knack of it. There have been times when I could have used it to good effect on clients.'

'Have you any idea where we are?' asked Avery.

Tom shrugged. 'Hawaii, Tahiti, Tonga—you pays your penny and you takes your choice.'

'We're not on Earth,' said Avery with sudden conviction.

'Come again?'

'I said we're not on Earth.'

'Now look here, old man. Don't get too imaginative. It's been a very peculiar experience, I agree. But one mustn't let the balance of one's judgement be disturbed.'

'Don't talk rot,' retorted Avery irritably. 'I presume you had the same kind of experience as I did—roof dissolving into stars, and then an inscrutable message from a heavenly voice?'

Tom smiled. 'It seems so.'

'Well, I have news for you,' said Avery, determined to break through the barrier of smugness. 'I was not too busy having hysteria to notice that the stars weren't our stars.'

'What precisely do you mean, old man?'

Avery's nerves were on edge, and he didn't much care for the 'old man' bit. It was just too public school to be true. 'I mean,' he said evenly, 'that the constellations were not terrestrial constellations—old man.'

'Are you a bloody astronomer?'

'No, but I have eyes in my head.'

Tom did a bit of rapid thinking. 'So what? We live—perhaps I should say lived—in the northern hemisphere, old chap. The stuff we saw may be stars that are way down under.'

'I've seen the southern hemisphere constellations,' persisted Avery, 'and I'm reasonably familiar with them. . . . What *I* saw just didn't belong.'

'Hell,' said Tom, 'don't try to frighten me—and for the love of Mike don't start a panic when the girls are finally with us. The sun looks normal enough, the sea looks normal enough. . . . Take my word for it, we may be in foreign parts, but we are still on dear old terra firma.'

Avery's irritation dissolved in his amusement at what he considered to be Tom's ostrich-like attitude. 'The terra may be firm enough, but it isn't our terra—that's the only point I'm making.'

'You've fallen for the treatment,' said Tom complacently. 'For reasons unknown, some nit has dumped us in the South Pacific—or some equivalent region. I can tell you one thing. There's going to be fun when I get back home. Habeas corpus and all that rot.'

'Hello, people, I've arrived.' The welcome interruption was provided by Barbara sitting up and regarding them both brightly. 'What was that somebody was saying about the South Pacific?'

Tom shot Avery a warning glance, then he grinned cheerily at Barbara. 'Glad you feel able to join the party at last. . . . I was just pointing out to Richard that in all probability we have been dumped somewhere in the South Pacific.'

Barbara yawned and shook her head. 'Grow up, lover boy. Richard is right. We're elsewhere.'

Avery raised an eyebrow. 'How long have you been awake?'

'Long enough. . . . A girl likes to know what kind of party she's joining before becoming an active member.' She stood up, stretched, then peered at Mary. 'The sleeping beauty is still out. Ah, youth! Ah, carefree youth!'

'You're both crazy,' persisted Tom. 'They haven't been able to send a man to Mars, yet—so I don't see how they could pop this little expedition down somewhere in the deep blue yonder.'

'They?' echoed Barbara. 'Who do you mean by *they*?'

'Boffins—the space wallahs.'

'My dear, dear Tom,' said Barbara sweetly, 'do me a small favour and stop talking like something out of the book of the film. . . . Incidentally, I know something you don't. Try looking over your shoulder—in the sky. . . . A little higher. . . . Now a little to the left.'

He stared for a moment or two then became aware of a faint silvery crescent—high, remote, almost lost in the blueness.

'The moon,' said Tom finally. 'So what. The moon in daytime is a perfectly normal phenomenon. See it a lot in summer. In the South Pacific the seasons and daylight appearance will be reversed, that's all.'

'Perhaps,' said Barbara. 'Now look low over that bunch of palm trees.'

Tom looked. So did Avery. There was a long silence.

'Jesus!' said Tom. He sat down heavily on the camp bed and fumbled shakily for another cigarette. 'Stone me! This is bloody ridiculous. It's—it's. . . . ' Words quite definitely failed him.

Avery looked at Barbara. 'You're very observant,' he said, 'and very self-composed.'

'It takes more than a couple of moons to give me the vapours,' retorted Barbara. 'Besides, hasn't it struck you as rather odd how calm and reasonable we're being after recent experiences? Especially that last one.' She shuddered. 'I was screaming for mercy at the end of it. And now here I am, cool as anything, dumped on a bloody alien sea-shore, counting the number of moons in the sky and taking away the number I first thought of. . . . If you ask me, they not only slipped us the crystal, they also slipped us a pretty good tranquillizer.'

Avery thought that one over. 'It's more than possible,' he admitted. 'By all the laws we ought to be pretty shattered. To tell the truth, I feel remarkably tranquil. . . . I just hope to hell it doesn't wear off.'

'It will,' said Barbara grimly. 'I just want someone to be there to catch me when it does, that's all.'

'Where—where am I?' Mary suddenly sat up, with a dazed look on her face.

'I never thought to hear those immortal words!' exclaimed Barbara joyously. 'Relax, ducky. You are among friends. The unhappy look on Tom's face is simply due to the fact that he has just seen a couple of spare moons. Tom is very orthodox. He finds the situation a wee bit upsetting.'

Mary stood up cautiously. She gazed at the sand and the sea. Then she said suddenly: 'This is very silly, I know, but at the moment I'm ravenously hungry.'

Avery surveyed the pile of camping equipment and the four neatly stacked cabin trunks. 'Well, let's see what we can find. Whoever was responsible for this lot seems to have thought of just about everything. I just hope he, she or—more probably it—didn't forget to include food.'

'Look!' said Barbara, pointing to a small cloth-covered basket. 'Three will get you five it's a picnic breakfast.'

Avery smiled. 'No takers. This just about fits the absurd logic of the situation.'

It was indeed a picnic breakfast—of a kind. Chicken and ham sandwiches, bottles of milk, a thermos flask of coffee—and a bottle of champagne.

Tom looked at the champagne in awe. 'This beats the celestial band. Nothing is real any more. We're all cutting out regulation-size paper dolls in a psychiatric ward somewhere in London.'

'Don't open it,' said Avery. 'I have a feeling there is going to be a time when we really need that champagne.'

Barbara pulled a face. 'I need it now.'

'No you don't. You need some nice, wholesome milk. It's going to be a long day.'

'There's something else,' said Mary, taking an envelope from the bottom of the basket. It was a thick brown envelope. She opened it and slipped the contents out on to her bed. There was a number of thin pieces of plastic, each about post-card size and each bearing a coloured picture of an animal, a fish or a plant together with a few lines of text in English.

Avery picked one of them up and gazed at it curiously. It showed an animal. A long and rather ferocious-looking hybrid of snake and lizard that was basking by a small pool with its tail hanging in the water. *This creature is dangerous,* said the text. *In habits it is similar to the terrestrial crocodile. The flesh is not good for eating.*

Mary was looking at a slip of paper that she had found among the plastic pictures.

'Listen to this,' she said, her voice shaking a little. '*From now on you will be required to find your own food and to ensure your own survival. The environment in which you have been placed is not abnormally hostile to human life. It is hoped that you will orientate successfully and derive something of value from the experience.*'

The four of them looked at each other. Suddenly and strangely, the nightmare had become real. Too real.

'Jesus H. Christ!' exploded Tom. His mouth opened again, but the words seemed unwilling to come out.

'Oh, well, who's for breakfast?' said Barbara, with an attempt at brightness.

Mary vainly tried to hold back a flow of treacherous tears. 'I—I'm not really hungry any more.'

'Eat!' said Avery in a surprisingly harsh voice. 'We're all going to eat. And then we'll decide what we are going to do. I don't know where the hell we are, or what we're supposed to be doing, but I'm going to stay alive. With all the crazy things that have been happening it's more than a matter of survival, now. It's a matter of principle. . . . Somebody or something is playing very elaborate games with us. If for nothing else, I'm going to live long enough to reverse the process.'

He stared moodily at the sea-shore. A few moments ago it had seemed attractively unreal—almost like the setting for a romantic piece of nonsense in cinemascope. But now an invisible shadow loomed obscurely over the whole bright morning. The fiction had been switched into a peculiar reality. And even the sunlight had become sinister.

SEVEN

NOBODY FELT LIKE CHAMPAGNE. But they sat down and ate the sandwiches and drank the milk. It seemed to be the most sensible thing to do.

When he began to eat, Avery discovered that he was actually hungry. Eating was a practical operation: it inspired practical thoughts. While he disposed of the sandwiches he glanced through some of the plastic pictures.

There was a fruit like a pear which, according to the caption, was palatable and rich in food value. There was also a sort of six-legged rabbit which was supposed to taste like lamb. And another animal that seemed like a cross between a wild boar and a miniature rhinoceros. This was reported as being both dangerous and edible. It looked to Avery like the sort of animal it would be wise to avoid completely.

Altogether, there were about fifty pictures. Presently they would have to be classified. Presently everyone would have to memorize them as completely as possible—especially the ones of the dangerous creatures. . . .

He glanced at the shore which had seemed so friendly and now looked so desolate. It was a surprisingly even strip of whitish sand, varying between about thirty and about seventy yards wide. The high-water mark was easily discernible by a ragged line of sea-debris—weeds, driftwood and even a few entire tree trunks. About ten yards behind this the trees and forest began—the great green enigma of land.

Soon they would have to explore, thought Avery. He did not relish the prospect. On earth, anywhere on earth, one might form a rough idea of what to expect. But here, on a planet where two moons and one sun swam lazily through a sky that was tremendously and intensely blue—here, after a star voyage that defeated the imagination and that had been made for a purpose completely outside the range of human experience—here it would be suicidal to expect anything less than the unexpected.

However, the first thing to do was to establish a temporary camp, to make a secure base—or, at least, a base that was as secure as possible, bearing in mind that nothing at all was known about the place. Apart from the fact that it contained some rather unusual flora and fauna. . . .

He became aware that Barbara was talking to him.

'In the cereal packets that used to grace my breakfast table back in the dear dead days of sanity,' she said, 'they used to give away model spacemen. They all wore armoured suits with goldfish bowls on top.'

He smiled. 'Fortunately, we don't need space suits here. The air is a damned sight more breathable than it is—or was—in London. And it's a lot warmer, too.'

'The point I'm making,' went on Barbara, 'is that all the spacemen were different types. There was a geologist, an engineer and a lot of others. I tried to collect the set, but there was always one that evaded me. It said on the packet that he was the vital one—the leader of the expedition. . . . I've an idea that's what we could use here.'

'Be adult,' said Tom gloomily. 'There isn't any expedition. Only four displaced people.' He laughed mirthlessly. 'And I mean displaced.'

'For better or worse,' retorted Barbara, 'we're the expedition. And somebody has to be responsible for us, otherwise we'll go round in ever-decreasing circles.'

'Barbara is right,' agreed Mary. 'Somebody has to make the decisions.'

'A man,' added Barbara.

Avery said: 'That narrows the field somewhat.'

Barbara grinned. 'Perhaps more than you might think.'

Tom didn't seem to care for the idea. 'We don't need a fuehrer. As mature people—I hope—we ought to be able to discuss problems and work them out together.'

'A committee of four,' observed Barbara, 'is not going to be much use in an emergency.'

'We don't have any emergencies yet. Meanwhile, why not be entirely democratic?'

'Because, my dear Tom, the emergency is of now—for indefinite duration.'

'I'm afraid she's right,' said Avery. 'One of us is going to have to be a benevolent despot, at least for a while. If you'd like to take on the job, you are welcome. I imagine whoever has it is going to be rather unpopular at times.'

'Just a moment,' said Barbara. 'You've forgotten the electorate. Mary and I ought to have a say in this.'

Tom sighed. 'Let's not make it too much like Gilbert and Sullivan. . . . What about a trial period for the dictatorship—say three days?'

'That sounds reasonable,' said Mary. 'If we don't like the way it works, we can try something else.'

Avery smiled. 'That's fine. The only point is that we don't know how long a day is—by our standards.'

'What do you mean?' Mary was puzzled.

'Depending on the rotation of the planet, it could be quite a bit longer than twenty-four hours or even less. We'll have to time it.'

'Since we're playing games,'' said Tom drily, 'you can be the leader of the expedition. I hope you brought your cereal packet complete with printed instructions.'

'That's settled, then,' said Barbara. 'Now we're in business.'

'One moment.' Avery was by no means sure it was settled. 'You'd better know what you are in for. *If* I take on any responsibility, I expect you all to do what I ask you to do—and do it willingly. You may think I'm asking you to do the wrong thing. Then say so. But if I still say you do it, then it has to be done. . . . I'm sorry, but I don't think that we can play it any other way at this stage. Is that understood?'

'Sieg Heil!' said Tom. Nevertheless, he seemed relieved.

Avery smiled. 'The concentration camps will come later. . . . Now, here is the first edict: nobody is to go out of sight. Is that clear? The reason is obvious. We don't know what dangers there are, so we expose ourselves to the minimum risk until we find out.'

Barbara said: 'There are certain things that ladies—and gentlemen—have to do out of sight.'

'Not any more, there aren't,' said Avery emphatically. 'At least, not yet. We'll get a latrine going as soon as possible. Meanwhile just find your own piece of sand and stay in view.'

Barbara grinned. 'I'm afraid this little piggy can't wait any longer. I'll be back in a minute.' She retreated about thirty yards, lowered her slacks and panties and calmly squatted on the sand.

The others pointedly ignored her; but they were conscious that the act itself—though trivial and entirely natural—had somehow demolished in a single moment all the accepted and sophisticated habits of civilization. It was oddly and incongruously symbolic.

When she came back, she said rather bravely: 'That feels better, I must say.'

Tom looked shocked. So did Mary. Avery felt that the gesture needed to be underlined. There was no room for coyness now. They were going to have to live in close proximity and get used to it.

'I could do with a good piss myself,' he remarked deliberately. Then he, too, walked a few yards away. He unbuttoned his trousers and urinated vaguely towards the sea.

'Well, now,' said Tom brightly, when he returned to the group, 'since we're getting so broad-minded, how about a general sex orgy just to pass the time?'

'There is no time left to pass,' remarked Avery, unsmiling, 'because everyone is about to go to work.' He surveyed the litter of camping equipment. 'Priority number one—weapons. Let's see what we can find in this jumble.'

'Weapons?' Mary seemed confused.

'Yes, anything—knives, clubs—anything. We may just possibly have to defend ourselves at short notice. So we'll need to have something handy. Later, no doubt, we can devise a few gadgets of our own.'

'In my little box,' said Tom, glancing at the pile of cabin trunks, 'there is a thirty-eight revolver and fifty rounds.' He seemed embarrassed. 'Don't know how it got there. I used to keep it in the flat."

'Excellent!' said Avery. 'Which is your box?'

'Ah, that's the question.' Tom stared at the pile. All the trunks were identical. 'It'll be the bottom one, I expect. . . . Finagle's Second Law.'

It was indeed the bottom one. The trunks were heavy, and it was all that Tom and Avery could do to lift them.

'Just what is Finagle's Second Law?' asked Barbara, as Tom knelt down and rummaged for the revolver and ammunition.

He looked up at her and grinned. 'Finagle's Second Law states that if anything can go wrong in a given situation, it invariably will. . . . Ah, here's the cannon.' He handed it and the box of ammunition to Avery.

Avery inspected the gun, broke open the box of ammunition and inserted six shells in the chamber. He snapped the chamber back into position. 'Hang on to your hats. I'm going to test this thing.' He fired out to sea. The report was flat, almost muffled, but it made everyone jump a little. 'That's O.K., then.' He broke the chamber out, and replaced the round he had used. Then he gave the revolver back to Tom. 'Hang on to this for the time being. . . . I'd be glad if you'd make a sort of preliminary reconnaissance, just around where we are. Don't go out of sight or shouting distance.

Take a look at the vegetation and see what you can make of it. Come back in about quarter of an hour.'

'Aye-aye, skipper.' Tom saluted ironically, and wandered off with the revolver held loosely in his hand.

Avery watched him saunter leisurely along the beach. He had a feeling that, sooner or later, there would probably be difficulties with Tom. But now was not the time to anticipate possible or imaginary problems. There were quite enough real ones to be going on with.

'Look what I've found,' said Mary. She had been delving into the camping gear and had unearthed a bundle of four sheathed knives and a couple of light hatchets. Each of the sheaths was attached to a leather belt.

Avery inspected them, then buckled one of the belts round his waist. 'Daggers will be worn by everyone this season,' he said. 'It's the latest fashion.'

Barbara grimaced. 'Don't you think we are carrying this security ploy a bit too far?'

'Possibly. I'd rather be nervous and alive than nonchalant and dead. . . . If you ever have to use these things for other than carving steaks, try to hold the knife like this and strike upwards. You stand a better chance of penetrating.'

'Lift up your hearts,' observed Barbara solemnly. 'What next?'

'Camp One is next. I think we ought to make it fairly near to the trees, a bit beyond that line of driftwood. We'll find somewhere better when we know a bit more about this place. How many tents are there?'

'Four,' said Mary. 'They look as if they will be fairly big ones.'

'Good. You two stay here and try to sort out the immediate things we're going to need—cooking utensils, blankets, if any, and stuff like that—and I'll just take a look at that piece of high ground.' He gestured towards a small rise about fifty yards away. 'If it looks all right, we'll move all the stuff there when Tom gets back. . . . Where is he, by the way?'

They looked along the beach, but Tom was nowhere to be seen. They looked for about a minute, but there was only a set of footprints fading away towards the trees.

'Idiot!' said Avery irritably. 'I told him to stay in sight.'

'Ought we to look for him?' asked Barbara.

'No. At least, not yet.'

As if to comment upon Avery's answer, there came the sound of a single shot—not apparently very far away. Mary and Barbara looked startled.

'Damn!' exploded Avery. He was worried. Not entirely irrelevantly he found himself thinking about what Tom had called Finagle's Second Law. But the pessimism was unjustified.

Presently, Tom emerged from the trees and came towards them. He was carrying something. As he came closer, Avery saw that it was a six-legged 'rabbit' such as was illustrated in the set of plastic pictures. Tom seemed very pleased with himself.

'Home is the hunter,' he said, flinging the furry corpse at Barbara's feet. 'That should make the basis of a decent stew. . . . Shot from the hip at about ten paces. Not bad, eh?'

'We now have forty-eight left,' said Avery coldly.

'Forty-eight what, old man?'

'Rounds of ammunition.'

'Oh. . . . I see. . . . Still, you popped one off at the ocean, didn't you?'

'Would you have preferred not to know whether the gun worked?'

Tom ignored the question. 'Never fired the thing before. What a wheeze! I got it for twenty-two marks fifty in Frankfurt and gave myself a rare thrill smuggling it through the Customs at dear old London Airport. I must say it's quite a nice little toy.'

'Give it to me,' said Avery.

'Why should I?'

'Because I say so.'

'Not good enough, old man. Go play fuehrer by yourself.'

Avery hit him. He was surprised himself at the speed and strength of the blow—a hand-edge chop to the neck that brought Tom down like a sack of potatoes. Fortunately, Tom was too surprised to hang on to the revolver. Avery picked it up quickly—and at the same time cursed himself for being a bloody fool. This was a fine start to building up mutual trust.

He wanted to apologize to Tom, who sat grunting on the sand and massaging his neck. He was on the point of helping him to his feet and finding a few conciliatory words, when Mary spoke.

'Need you be so—so brutal, Richard?'

'Yes,' he said, killing the apology that was almost on his lips. 'I told him to look around, so he starts shooting things. I told him to give me the gun, but he doesn't. . . . I'm just doing the job you gave me to do—my way.'

Barbara went to help Tom to his feet. 'You're both a couple of fatheads,' she said. 'But Richard is right—in a wrong sort of way. Now stop it, the pair of you.'

Avery held out his hand. Surprisingly, Tom took it. Then he pulled Avery forward and hit him in the stomach. Winded though he was, Avery didn't let go of the gun. He buckled up, gasping.

'Two can play at this game,' said Tom. 'How does it feel to be on the receiving end?' He seemed rather pleased with himself.

'Not nice,' panted Avery. But oddly he was glad. It had restored Tom's self-respect. They were equal once more.

'I'd like my revolver back,' went on Tom. But he sounded more like somebody who was making a point rather than a request.

'Sorry,' said Avery, scrambling to his feet. 'You're not getting it. Perhaps I shouldn't have hit you, but that doesn't alter matters. You don't get the gun until I know I can rely on you.'

Tom grinned. 'You may not live that long.'

Suddenly Mary spoke. 'You're behaving like spoiled children. Heaven knows what Barbara and I are going to do if we have to rely on people like you.'

Avery shrugged. 'Well said. . . .Now let's get on with the job. Tom, you and I must find a spot suitable for pitching camp while they sort out the necessary gear. . . . Do you know anything about camping?'

'Used to be a scout, old man.' The 'old man' was emphasized.

'Fine, you've just been appointed camp-maker extraordinary. Come on.'

The piece of high ground that Avery had noticed was not suitable. Tom pointed out its flaws, chief of which was the problem of drainage. But about a hundred yards farther along the beach there was a hillock with a flat, almost circular top covered by fine grass. It also had the advantage of being close to a small stream.

'This will do,' said Tom, after a critical inspection. 'For a start, anyway. We can find somewhere better in the fullness of time.'

Avery gazed back along the way they had come. 'I suppose we ought to begin the business of fetching and carrying, then.'

EIGHT

THE DAY GREW WARMER. Presently, the two men stripped to the waist. Despite its weight and the fact that it was rubbing a raw patch on the side of his leg, Avery kept the revolver in his trousers pocket. Tom carried one of the sheath knives.

Avery, conscious of the fact that it was necessary to reduce the hostility between them, took care to consult Tom on all aspects of camp making, and deferred to most of his suggestions—though it soon became clear that Tom's camping lore was hardly any better than his own.

Although the two women helped as much as possible, it took nearly a couple of hours before the tents, equipment and cabin trunks had been moved to what was beginning to be called Camp One. The trunks were the hardest to move. In the end, the men were reduced to dragging each one, yard by yard, across the soft sand and shingle.

Camp One, thought Avery, as they began to put up a couple of tents, was a good and symbolic title. It indicated the possibility of Camp Two, and so on. In short, the inference was that they were not just going to sit down—a static group of castaways—and consider their grievances. Of course, there was nothing at all that could be done about the most important problem—getting back home. But it was just possible, if contact could be established with the people—or creatures—who had brought them here, that some kind of solution could be worked out. So far, all the evidence seemed to indicate that the kidnappers—whoever or whatever they were—had pretty important reasons for engaging in such an elaborate project. One of the first steps, decided Avery, when he had time to think would be to try to work out intelligently what those reasons were. If that could be done, it might lead to a way of frustrating the project and/or striking a bargain. The possibility looked rather remote, but at least it was a possibility. Meanwhile, there was no time to think things out carefully. There was too much work to be done.

The tents were each large enough to accommodate two people in reasonable comfort; and so Avery decided that for the time being only two of them would be used domestically—one for the women and one for the men. Another tent would be used as a shelter for the supplies, and the remaining one would be kept in reserve.

Having erected the tents—again a symbolic as well as a practical operation—Avery left the task of sorting out the stores and making the accommodation as comfortable as possible to Mary and Barbara. The next problem was what to do about defence. Although the only wild life in evidence so far had been the six-legged 'rabbit' shot by Tom, the set of little plastic pictures indicated the existence of several dangerous creatures. It would certainly not be pleasant, for example, to wake up one night and find one of those miniature pig-like rhinoceros things poking its nose into a tent. . . .

Tom's mind was working along the same lines.

He dumped the bundle of sleeping bags he had been carrying and wiped the sweat from his forehead. 'What are we going to do about the bug-eyed monsters?' he asked. 'Can't have the girls crawling up a wall because some dear little five-foot lizard wants to be friendly.'

'Great minds,' remarked Avery, leaving the platitude unfinished. 'I think we are going to have to build a fence of some kind.'

'Tall order. What about keeping a fire going all night?'

'That too.' Avery smiled. 'But the animals here may be a little different from the ones on earth. They may even like a fire. We shall just have to find out.'

Tom was silent for a while. At length he said: 'The trunks seem reasonably weatherproof. If we take out the kind of things we're likely to need in the immediate future; and then lay the trunks end to end round the back of the tents, they ought to make a fairly substantial part of a barrier. . . . What do you think?'

'They certainly ought to be used until we can find something better. We'll have to complete the circle with driftwood—and we'll want a stack of that for the fire, as well.' Avery took the revolver out of his pocket and felt the sore patch on his leg gingerly. He put the gun into one of the tents. 'I'm tired of lugging that thing around with me,' he said, watching Tom carefully.

'All hands have to go armed,' remarked Tom drily. 'The Fuehrer's personal orders.'

'The Fuehrer will wear a knife,' retorted Avery. Tom made no move to claim the gun. Presently the two of them went to collect driftwood. The sun glared fiercely down.

They came back hot, weary and loaded about half an hour later. Finding driftwood of a suitable size had not been as easy as Avery had hoped.

They saw Barbara and Mary sitting in front of the tents, sipping water from plastic tumblers.

'That's something I should have thought about,' said Avery, licking his dry lips. 'How do we know it's fit to drink?'

'I found a canvas bucket,' said Mary. 'It had a box of pills inside. The instructions said to dissolve one pill in each gallon of drinking water.'

'I see. About how many pills are there?'

'I don't know. Five hundred. Perhaps a thousand. See for yourself.' She gave him the box. Avery did a rough count of the top layer and then an even rougher multiplication sum. He thought the answer came to nearer two thousand.

'How does the water taste?'

'Like Vichy water,' said Barbara. 'It's got a pleasant sort of tingle. Try some. You both look as if you need it.' She got two more tumblers and poured from the canvas bucket.

Avery sipped some of the water, rolled it round his mouth and swallowed. For a split second, the entire landscape seemed to ripple slightly—as if he were drinking some kind of alcohol with an immediate and powerful kick. Then the ripple froze back into reality, and it was as if colours and shapes were even sharper than before.

Barbara was right. It did taste a bit like Vichy water. But, perhaps because of the strenuous work they had been doing, it seemed the most refreshing liquid he had ever drunk.

'Quite a wallop!' said Tom with enthusiasm. He drained his tumbler and held it out for more.

It was then that Mary screamed.

Avery dropped the tumbler and whipped round, his knife miraculously already in his hand. Out of the corner of his eye he saw—and was enormously reassured by it—that Tom was in a similar, half-crouching position, with his knife ready to strike as well. They gazed towards the trees, about twenty yards away, at which Mary was staring and pointing. There was nothing.

'I—I saw a man!'

Still there was nothing. They all stared in silence for a few seconds. Then Barbara broke the tension.

'Never scream at men, honey. It tends to give them a bad impression.'

'What was he like?' asked Avery, still keeping his eyes on the trees.

'Tall, golden hair, very solid looking.'

'That wasn't a man. That was a vision,' said Barbara. 'The spring water seems to be more potent than you'd think.'

'I did see him,' persisted Mary.

Avery looked at her. She looked rather shaken, but she did not seem like the sort of girl who might be inclined to have visions of tall golden men. 'What was he wearing?' asked Avery.

'Nothing—I think.'

Tom snorted. 'That's just about all we need—a bloody naked Adonis lurking in the background.'

'Do you know whether he was armed or not?' went on Avery.

'He didn't seem to be. But—but it was all so quick. . . . I think he was just as surprised as I was.'

Avery thought that at least a token investigation was called for. 'Tom, you and I will go and take a look. If there *was* somebody, he is probably half a mile away by now; but I suppose we had better try to make a thorough search of all possible cover within range of about a hundred yards.' He turned to Barbara. 'I parked the revolver in the tent here. You'd better get it and keep your eyes skinned while we're gone. Don't use it unless you absolutely have to.'

The search took quite a long time. Nobody saw anything. By the time they got back to camp, Avery was feeling tired, and irritable. He saw the smoke rising from the fire that Barbara and Mary had made, and was unreasonably angry.

'Who the devil told you to make a fire. It can be seen for miles.'

Barbara gazed at him coolly. 'No one, actually. I just used my own little brains.'

'You didn't use them very well, then. Tom and I collected that driftwood to make a fence, not a bloody picnic fire.'

'I assumed,' said Barbara, 'that you would not care to eat your meat raw. Perhaps I should have enquired more closely into your tastes.'

Someone had skinned and dismembered the 'rabbit', and Mary was busy roasting parts of it on a couple of sticks. Someone had also been collecting fruit. There was a small pile of what looked like grapefruit and some extraordinarily large pears. Someone, in fact, had been busy.

'Sorry,' said Avery. 'My nerves are on edge.'

'Don't mention it,' said Barbara. 'Incidentally, I checked the fruit with our coloured cigarette cards. The pears are supposed to be very nutritious, and the others are thirst-quenchers. At least we shan't starve to death. About every tenth tree has fruit of some kind.'

The pieces of rabbit were spitting and sizzling as Mary, with sweat pouring down her face, doggedly turned them over the embers of the tiny fire. The smell of cooking meat that assailed Avery's nostrils was positively enchanting.

Mary sighed. 'Lunch is about ready. You can have roast fingers as well, if you like.'

'Hang on a second,' said Barbara. 'I'll get plates and cutlery. We might as well keep it as civilized as possible.' She laid four plates neatly on the ground in front of one of the tents.

The rabbit tasted good—not like terrestrial rabbit, but still good. It had quite a strong flavour, but its flesh was very tender.

As they sat in front of the tents at this, their first meal that could come under the heading of 'living off the country', Avery marvelled at the unreal normality of it all. Not so long ago they had been living in London in a bleak February. They had been strangers. Perhaps they had even passed each other in the street; or during the rush hour maybe a couple of them had been pushed together in the Underground. Yet now they were no longer strangers: they had been collectively banded—was that the right word?—light-years away from Earth in a conspiracy of survival.

Avery began to try to take stock of his companions. Tom was the kind of man with whom, he knew, he had very little in common. If the two of them had been brought together somehow in the old days—funny how one already began to think in terms of the old days—they would have taken an instant dislike to each other and would probably have avoided any further meeting. But now, depending upon each other, each of them was going to have to adapt. Avery would have to get used to Tom's silly jokes, his little *bonhomie* and his little stupidities. Tom, he supposed, would also have to adjust to Avery's irritability, his impatience and what, trying to be objective, he regarded as his own colourless personality. Yet, in an odd sort of way, Tom seemed reliable. He seemed to possess a combination of stubbornness and staying power. Within the limitations of his vaguely adolescent approach, he could be a useful character. Avery remembered the moment when Mary had screamed. Tom had not stood by with a foolish look on his face. He had been ready to fight. And if there had been cause to fight, doubtless he would have given a pretty good account of himself.

As for the women, well, they were more complex characters than Tom. Or, perhaps, thought Avery, it was just that all women seemed complex to him—all except one. But he stopped that train of thought immediately. Now was not the time to think of Christine, even though recent experiences had somehow made her seem obscurely close.

He gave his attention to Barbara. Superficially, she was tough and capable. Superficially—and, indeed, so far all the evidence had supported this impression—she did not seem like the kind of woman who would have the vapours if things went badly. But, thought Avery, the toughness could be no more than a front—a mask which she had learned to present to a tough and unfriendly world. Underneath, he suspected, there was a different Barbara: a child looking for a lost doll, a little girl in search of security. . . .

Mary, perhaps, was the reverse—superficially fragile, yet with the kind of inward reserves that might, in the end, permit her to endure a great deal. Physically she was not as attractive or as exciting as Barbara, but her personality was more subtle, more intriguing. Perhaps there would come a time, especially if they were stuck here for long—God damn it! there was almost certain to come such a time—when sex problems would be the most important factor affecting the success or failure of their bid for survival. Avery didn't want any sex problems. He was even pretty sure that he didn't want any sex relationships. He was afraid of them. And he had been afraid for a long time. . . .

Suddenly, he realized that Tom was talking to him.

'Daydreaming, old sport? You haven't said a word in the last twenty minutes. You're not going into a decline, I trust.'

'Sorry, I was miles away. . . .That was a decent bit of meat, Tom. I'm glad you bagged it.'

'Permission to hunt for some more?'

Avery smiled. 'Yes, but not with the gun. We must try to keep that as a great deterrent.'

Mary stretched and sighed. She gazed up at the still clear sky, shading her eyes against the sun, which had apparently passed its zenith and was now fairly low over the sea. 'What a gorgeous climate this is. It's the one good thing about the whole situation. . . . I don't feel like doing a thing this afternoon. I just want to lie back and luxuriate.'

'No reason why you shouldn't, I suppose,' said Avery. 'But Tom and I will have to go after some more driftwood. There still isn't enough for a fence and a fire.'

'It still strikes me as remarkably odd,' observed Barbara, suppressing a yawn, 'that we aren't having fits of hysterics, gloom and despondency.'

'Simultaneously?' enquired Tom.

She laughed. 'Or in sequence—according to taste. The trouble is, how does one behave in a situation like this? I'm sure it hasn't been laid down in any book on etiquette. So I don't know whether to scream or relax.'

'There'll be plenty of time for screaming,' Avery assured her seriously, 'when we have made ourselves as safe and secure as possible. At the moment, I suspect we are both traumatized and sedated.'

'Big words,' scoffed Barbara. 'Big empty words. Meaning we don't know a damn thing. Maybe it's as well.'

There was silence for a minute or so. Silence wrapped in the even murmer of the sea.

At length, Avery said: 'Well, let's go after that wood. We want to get as much as possible before sunset.'

Barbara collected up the plates. 'Please, sir, may we bathe while you're away?'

Avery thought for a moment. 'No,' he said, 'definitely not. I'll think about it tomorrow. Hell, there's far too much to think about, as it is.'

NINE

SUNSET CAME WITH tropical suddenness. The evening meal was over—nothing but fruit, this time—and the fence, such as it was, was in position. One moment the world was still light and warm; and next moment, it seemed as if the sun had been completely swallowed by the sea. And a cool wind rustled through the trees, bearing with it an invisible tide of twilight and darkness.

The fence was less of a fence than a three foot high tangle of driftwood. It enclosed a few square yards containing two tents, four human beings and a fire. It enclosed a world within a world.

Avery looked at his companions in the firelight and wondered if they felt as lonely and exposed as he did. During the hours of daylight there had been so much to do, so much to think of doing, that there had been little opportunity for private thoughts and feelings. Daylight itself was a cloak of comfort; but now the cloak had been taken away, and there was a feeling of nakedness and fear.

The stars were coming out. Alien stars. Stars of another galaxy or perhaps just another part of Earth's galaxy. What an arrogant way to describe it—Earth's galaxy! It was related to the archaic thinking that had placed man at the fixed centre of the universe, sitting on a flat world, the one and only darling child of an anthropomorphic god.

But perhaps God had many children, and perhaps some of his children were adept at the manufacture of hypnotic crystals. And other things. . . .

Anyway, the stars were no less beautiful for being unfamiliar stars. They shone without warmth, without compassion. But that was part of the beauty; for they were the ultimate in detachment. Hydrogen bombs, London winters, human hopes and fears—even interstellar abduction—were as nothing to those bright needle points of eternity.

Avery felt that it was going to be a long time before he could come to terms with his predicament. He could already accept it as a fact—in so far as any of the facts of recent experience had proved acceptable—but he could not yet accept it emotionally. London, evidently, was light-years away. That, in itself, meant nothing. It might just as well be a few hundred or a few thousand miles over the seaward horizon. Each was remote, in different ways, beyond the power of imagining.

What he could not accept was that, for all practical purposes, London both as a symbol and as a place had ceased to exist. Intellectually, he knew that the chances of seeing it—or Earth—again were very low. Yet the rattle of the Underground was still in his ears, the subtle throb of the city seemed to find an echo even in his pulse. He wondered what would happen to him if or when he abandoned hope—not a specific hope, but the curious, almost unformed hope that some day, once again, he would belong. For the first time, he was surprised to discover, mankind felt to him like a great family. It was an odd sensation, this knowledge of being a child, lost and far from home. But he was not entirely cut off from mankind; for he had the company of three people. Looking at them, he wondered what kind of confusions were whirling round in their heads.

Barbara had a bottle of whisky. In fact, Barbara had about six dozen bottles of whisky. Her cabin trunk had been lined with them just as Avery's had been lined with cigarettes. Somehow, he had not thought that she would be a heavy drinker. It was not, as she had carefully explained when the bottle was produced, that she was an alcoholic or even 'in a sordid state'. It was just that she had needed a crutch on which to lean in a world where she had had to endure an unending role as a TV immortal in a hospital that looked as if it would go on admitting imaginary patients until the entire population was neurotic, bed-ridden or both.

Barbara sat with Tom in front of the tent that he referred to brightly as 'the girls' dorm'. They each had tumblers—and the whisky. Mary and Avery sat less than a couple of yards away, but enough to make it a gap, outside 'the men's dorm'. Avery also nursed a whisky—a small one. But Mary had steadfastly refused to drink. She looked at Barbara somewhat anxiously. Barbara was on her third generous double, but so far there did not appear to be much effect. Tom, however, was looking rather melancholy. He had matched her, glass for glass.

For a little while, there had been a lull in the conversation. But the spell was broken when Avery threw a handful of wood on the fire and sent a shower of sparks up towards the sky.

Barbara let out a deep sigh, shook her head, then

said abruptly: 'We're going to have to have a naming of names.'

'I beg your pardon?' Avery was bewildered.

'The flora and fauna, stupid. All those pretty pictures tell us what the animals and plants are like in these parts, and what they're good—or bad—for. But they don't have any names. I think it's very important for animals to have names. Besides, how the hell do we talk about them if they don't?'

'She's got a point,' said Tom solemnly. 'Damn confusing to pop off at a six-legged rabbit when it isn't a rabbit, if you see what I mean.'

'You're drunk,' said Mary primly.

Tom laughed. 'The Leith police dismisseth us.' He delivered himself of the tongue-twister safely, and with as much satisfaction as a scientist propounding a new and revolutionary theory.

'Simple. It's a rabbitype,' announced Barbara.

'What is?'

'A six-legged rabbit. It's a rabbitype. There's also a rhinotype, a crocotype and a doggotype, etcetera, etcetera, *ad nauseam*.'

Avery smiled. 'That's nice and convenient. But how would you describe the Greek god that Mary saw? Incidentally there doesn't appear to be a picture card to tell us what *he* does.'

'Simple,' said Barbara. 'He's either a supertype or a sexotype,' she giggled, 'depending upon your sex, how you look at him, and what he does to you.'

'I hope,' retorted Avery, 'that he doesn't do anything at all—if he exists.'

'He exists, all right,' said Mary. She shivered. 'I wish you hadn't reminded me of him.'

'Darling,' said Tom, 'Richard and I will protect

your virginity, even unto the last drop of whisky . . . . Christ, I'm tired! It must be the sea air.'

'The "type" suffix will do quite nicely for the time being,' decided Avery. 'And incidentally, a priority task for us all is memorizing those pictures and the information. It may mean the difference between survival or otherwise. . . . Touching on Tom's last remark, it may be a good idea if you three went to bed. It's been a pretty tiring sort of day.'

'We three?' said Barbara. 'What are *you* going to do?'

'Take the first watch and keep the fire going. I'll waken you in a couple of hours. Then you can do a spell and waken Tom. Mary can have what I hope will be the dawn watch.'

Tom stretched. 'Beddibyes is a lovely and almost holy thought—providing it's a bed with four legs in West One. Somehow, a sleeping bag and a tent don't fill me with quite the same enthusiasm. However, when on Mars one must do as the dear little Martians do. Good night one and all. . . . Perhaps—if Barbara will be so kind—I'll just take a night-cap in with me.' He gave himself another generous measure of whisky.

'By the way,' said Avery, 'does your trunk contain any personal comforts—such as whisky or cigarettes?'

The question was addressed chiefly to Tom, but Mary answered it first. 'I have about half a hundredweight of sweets,' she confessed. 'I suppose I used to eat quite a lot, but—' she stopped. Even by firelight her blush was noticeable.

Avery transferred his gaze once more to Tom.

'Sorry, old man. There's nothing we can eat, drink or suck in my little box. All comforts, such as they are, are of a highly personal nature. . . .One assumes, of course, that civilized standards of privacy will not deteriorate in our little group. . . . Sweet dreams, everyone.' He disappeared inside the tent.

Avery was intrigued. There had seemed to be some tension in Tom's voice. Linking it up with that silly remark about privacy, it looked as if there was something he wanted to hide. But, clearly, in such a situation nothing could be hidden from anyone for long. Presently, they would all be painfully aware of each other's likes and dislikes, each other's strengths and weaknesses, each other's little secrets. . . . And, in a way, that would be another kind of nakedness. . . .

Mary was the next to go. A few minutes later she was followed into the tent by Barbara. Each of Avery's companions was still only two or three yards away, yet he felt suddenly and luxuriously alone.

He shivered a little, with cold and pleasure. Then he threw some more wood on to the fire and settled down to his vigil. Perhaps he ought to leave the camp and take a stroll round to see if there was anything about that was likely to 'go bump in the night'. But he dismissed the idea. It was now so dark that, away from the firelight, he would be able to see very little; but, at the same time, he would himself be more exposed. Better to stay put and rely on the fire and the fence.

He had been sitting by the fire for about three-quarters of an hour, immersed in his own thoughts and memories, when there was a movement by his side. It was Barbara—wearing a hastily thrown on shirt, a pair of slacks and nothing else.

'I can't sleep,' she whispered. 'I've tried all the

regulation positions and it won't work. Mary seems to have found the trick of it, though. She's well out.'

'Maybe you drank too much whisky.' Avery kept his own voice low.

She smiled. 'Or not enough. . . . Richard, I'm so bloodly lonely. Do me a favour, just hold my hand. Nothing else, that's all I need.'

Avery looked at her for a moment. Then he put one arm round her shoulder and drew her gently against his side. She let out a sigh of relief, and after a minute or two the tightness seemed to drain out of her body.

'It's wonderful,' she said, 'what a bit of human contact will do—actual physical contact, I mean. I was ready to twang like a harp, and now you are making me feel silly and relaxed.'

'Not too silly, I hope.'

Barbara gave him a curiously appraising look. 'No, not too silly. . . . It's early days yet, and we all have to be terribly adult about everything, haven't we?'

Avery had no answer to that, and she snuggled closer. After a time he found that they were almost clinging together; and that it gave him, too, a sense of security, a feeling of being slowly unwound. What was even more odd—and gratifying—was that the sex aspect didn't appear to obtrude at all.

'Why don't you go back to bed, now?' he asked at length.

'No thanks,' she murmured. 'This is better than sleeping.'

They sat there for a long time, not talking, hardly thinking, but just watching the fire and listening to the strange and intriguing night noises that were occasionally superimposed on the even sound of the sea.

TEN

THE NIGHT PASSED uneventfully. Two moons—one only very slightly larger than the other—drifted slowly like luminous balloons across a star-studded sky; and at last a red sun, curiously like Earth's sun, lifted above tree-tops already beginning to stream as a light dew evaporated.

Barbara and Avery had shared their watches, but Tom and Mary each took theirs alone. As it turned out, their vigils were rather short because Barbara and Avery did not turn in until less than a couple of hours before dawn. Though their sleep was brief it was remarkably refreshing; and at breakfast time they found it difficult to believe that they had spent most of the night huddled together by the fire. Avery, in fact, was mildly embarrassed by the memory. It seemed to imply the existence of an intimacy that he was not yet willing to accept.

Breakfast itself was a simple affair—the remainder of the fruit. Afterwards, Avery asked Tom to study the plastic pictures and then take himself off on a hunting expedition—without the gun.

Tom was in an uncooperative mood—possibly, thought Avery, as a result of last night's whisky. But, after delivering himself of a little speech on the entire uselessness of trying to catch 'game' with his bare hands, he made his departure. He spent some time looking for suitable throwing stones on the shore. Then he went inland. Avery did not set any limits to the hunt. He merely asked Tom to make sure he didn't get lost and to be back in about three hours. It was obvious that risks were going to have to be taken sometimes; and, since nothing dreadful had happened so far, Avery began to feel that the dangers might not be so great as he had imagined. He was worried still about the man Mary had seen. But to adopt an entirely defensive attitude seemed neither practical nor wise.

For himself, he decided upon a little exploration—along the shore. There was one problem particularly that he wanted to solve, though he realized that there was probably very little chance of solving it in a single day. The question was: had they been dumped on a relatively small island or a large land mass. There was, as yet, no way of telling; and although the answer did not seem to offer any special survival value, he felt it was important to know.

Before he departed on what could only be regarded as a preliminary survey, he gave clear and emphatic instructions to Mary and Barbara. They were not to go out of each other's sight. In fact they were to stay as close together as possible. If they went looking for more fruit, they must each carry a knife or hatchet and one of them must also have the gun. He repeated the standing order that the revolver must only be used in the last resort; if it was a question of survival. He also added the perhaps unnecessary advice that, if it came to shooting, whether it was man or beast, whoever had the gun must shoot to kill.

It was a bright warm morning when Avery

finally set off on his exploratory jaunt; and he began to feel optimistic. Not optimistic about anything particular, but simply about the remarkable and exciting fact of being alive. The sun was already a little higher than it had been on the previous day when he had awakened: and a rough and ready calculation indicated that a day on this planet lasted about twenty earth-hours.

Day One had, necessarily, been a bit of a shambles, he decided. Day Two must be used to increase both knowledge and self-reliance.

He had been walking along the shore for about half an hour when he came across the footprints. There were two sets—one larger than the other—possibly a man's and a woman's. They came from the direction of the trees to a small rocky pool, and then went back to the trees again, where they disappeared in the grass and undergrowth. The prints on the sand were clear and quite fresh-looking. Whoever had made them might still be in the vicinity.

Avery reconnoitred cautiously among the trees, but he found nothing. Presently, he returned to the rocky pool to see if he could find anything in the nature of a clue.

The pool itself was small and only a few yards from the high water mark on the stretch of sand. The strangers, evidently, had been kneeling for some time by the edge of the pool. There were marks where their toes must have dug into the sand; and four small patches of weed had been flattened.

Avery knelt carefully in two of the depressions to see what he could see. The pool contained several small fish and apparently nothing else but a few smooth round stones, each about the size of a large fist. But presently one of the stones moved, and Avery recognized it as a very ordinary looking crab. According to the set of plastic pictures, crabs were particularly good to eat. He wished now that he had brought something with which to catch them and to carry them. He did not care greatly for the prospect of using his hands.

He wondered guiltily whether he ought to go back to Camp One for a pan or a bucket. But finally he decided against it. Tom was on a hunting expedition. If he found nothing else, he would very likely come across some crabs.

Perhaps it was the search for food that had brought the strangers to this pool in the first place. Perhaps they would be coming back to it.

Avery stood up and looked about him uncertainly. Then, after a little hesitation, he decided to carry on with his survey. But the mood of optimism had evaporated. He began to feel anxious and exposed once more.

Suddenly, a thought struck him. Perhaps the Others (as he was beginning to think of them) were not indigenous but displaced persons as well! It would be absurdly comic if they were two groups of displaced terrestrials living now on a strange planet in fear of mutual discovery. But then he remembered Mary's description of the man she had seen. Somehow, it had not sounded like a description of a man who had recently been abducted: it had been more like the description of a man who was quite at home in his natural surroundings—a man who, perhaps, was justifiably surprised and annoyed at the intrusion of strangers.

Avery continued to walk along the beach, but he took care to stay close to the sea so that he could not easily be taken by surprise if someone happened to be watching him or following him behind the cover afforded by a green, luxuriant wall of vegetation.

Time passed. The morning wore on. Nothing happened. Avery's exploration took him past several small bays and round a fairly large headland. But there was still nothing to indicate whether he had covered a tiny stretch on a very long shore or had almost travelled round a very small island. He had an impression that the shore had a general tendency to bend more towards his right. Even so, the land could still be a relatively small bulge belonging to a very large mass.

He began to feel discouraged. For one thing, he wasn't being very scientific about the expedition. He should have been trying to plot his changes of direction by the sun, or something equally methodical. For another thing, he was beginning to feel anxious about Mary and Barbara. On reflection, it seemed to him that it had not been a good idea to leave the two women alone. Come to that, it probably wasn't even a good idea for him or Tom to wander off alone. Henceforth, he decided, and until they knew more about their surroundings, expeditions would be undertaken in pairs—one man and one woman. That would certainly be a safer arrangement.

Avery glanced at his watch and realized that he had been away from camp nearly two hours. It was time to go back. He had not intended to be away for more than three hours. He stopped and gazed intently at the shoreline ahead, which was visible for about half a mile before it bent once more to the right. He learned nothing—except that it was much the same as the miles of shore he had already walked over. Then he gazed seaward, scanning the horizon intently.

It was a clear morning. The sky was cloudless. High above, it was an intense blue; but where it came down to meet the sea it dissolved into a faintly misty purple. Avery stared at the purple fusion of sky and sea. For a moment, he thought he saw a far, vague outline of land. Then it dissolved. It came once more—and dissolved once more. It could be land or a low-lying bank of cloud—or just the strain of staring.

Reluctantly, Avery began to retrace his steps. He decided not to mention his mirage—if it was a mirage—to the others. Otherwise they might all begin seeing things to order. But, if it was real—if it was another piece of land—sooner or later someone else would see it. And anyway, if it was a piece of land, it was at least twenty miles away, probably much more. And without a boat, twenty miles of sea was—well, twenty miles of sea. . . . Of course, it should be possible to build a boat. . . .On the other hand, why waste time building boats and looking for more problems? The only worthwhile objective at the moment was to learn enough to stay alive. . . . His head was beginning to ache.

Suddenly, he stopped in his tracks and stared incredulously. He had almost reached the rocky pool where he had discovered signs of the Others. But it was not the pool that caught his attention, for it was now hidden.

It was hidden behind what seemed to be a monstrous, blinding, golden ball that was perhaps thirty yards in diameter and that looked as if it was poised to roll into the sea—from which it might even have emerged.

Avery stared at the shimmering, motionless

ball. It was so bright that his eyes began to smart, but he could not turn away. He felt the hysteria beginning to rise inside him—a tiny bubble of unreason expanding to such a pitch of tightness that it must presently burst.

It could be the sun, he thought idiotically. The sun could have fallen out of the sky, and now it's lying here on the sea-shore. It's not a great sphere of fire, it's a ball of liquid gold—and time has stopped, because I ought by now to have been burned to a cinder.

The sweat poured down his face, the smarting in his eyes became a sharp-edged pain; but a distant whisper of common sense told him that he was neither dead nor burning. His impulse to hysteria remained petrified at the point of explosion. After the first fantastic shock, his brain began to work once more.

The great ball was radiant and motionless. But there had to be some way in which it had got there. The one thing he did know was that it must have arrived less than an hour ago.

Despite the radiance, the curiously unreal sensation of tremendous heat, he forced himself to go a little closer, looking for tracks in the sand.

There were no tracks in the sand. There was not even a dent. The ball seemed to rest without weight, as if it was suspended at the end of an invisible rope. Cautiously, Avery walked round it. There was nothing—nothing but the pool and the footprints he had discovered earlier.

Then suddenly he heard a tiny, dry crackle—as of fine splinters of glass being broken. For a fraction of a second he thought he had simply imagined the sound. But at the same time the golden ball just disappeared.

It did not go up or away. It did not make any loud noise or create any turbulence in the air. What it did do was so utterly absurd as to give Avery serious doubts about his own sanity.

It simply faded.

A golden sphere, thirty yards in diameter, whose surface seemed to have the fluid iridescence of a massive globule of molten metal—to say nothing of the intense heat—just faded before his eyes. For a moment its outline appeared to vibrate intensely. Then it became transparent. And there was nothing.

Avery stood and stared. And blinked. The pain was going from his eyes. He felt drunk and unsteady and stupid and empty. He felt that he could no longer trust himself to think—just as he could certainly not trust himself to see.

There was no mark on the sand. Nothing had been disturbed, nothing at all. It was as if the mysterious sphere had never been.

That, of course, was the answer, he told himself reluctantly. After a couple of days or so as the prisoner of a computer in a spaceship and a night and a day on an island where it was possible to see two moons and six-legged rabbits, who would not be subject to visions?

Yet he did not really believe it was a vision, just as he did not really believe that the nebulous landshape he had seen on the horizon was a vision.

What then? Answer: he was going slightly—ever so gently and inevitably—clean out of his head. The leader of the expedition! Stark staring!

Anybody want to place bets on group survival, gents, with dear old demented Richard Avery running the show? Stand by to repel boarders, folks, we're being invaded by twenty-four-carat balloons. Never mind! All you have to do to cause the bastards to disappear up their own spherical arses is to make a noise like splinters of glass with schizophrenia.

Ah, that was it! The noise. Not splinters of glass. Static electricity. The crackle you get with a sweater when you take it off in a dry atmosphere. Rub two girl guides together in a dry climate and—

Christ, he thought. This won't do. I've got to dig a nice little, warm little, dark little hole representing sanity and bury the elasticated remnants of my mind in it before they go snapping off in a glorious bloody exeunt.

Maybe everything's an illusion. Maybe Barbara and Mary and Tom and two moons and an intelligence-testing computer and a skyful of alien stars have all come bursting out of my own sweet bullshitting unconscious mind. . . .

Maybe I'm in a lovely nut-house in London, and the next thing I know I'll be waking up after a long shot of electroshock to collect my season ticket for rugmaking. . . .

Barbara, Mary and Tom. He wanted to see them. He wanted to see them, touch them, talk to them as he had never wanted anything before in his life. Above all, he wanted the bitter security of not being alone.

He began to walk quickly, past the pool, back to camp. But he could not control himself. The walking became faster and faster. Then it became a headlong sprint. He was too old for that kind of pace. He had smoked too many cigarettes, he had let his body sag into a middle-aged bundle of bones and perished rubber. But he didn't care. Speed was the thing.

He ran until the very air seemed to grate like

gravel in his lungs. He ran until the pain in his chest was such that he expected his heart to literally break out like a tortured fugitive. He ran until the bright beach ahead began to darken and the forest and the sea swirled about him like green and turquoise mists that would presently close above his head and bury him in a warm sweet vapour of unbeing.

He ran until he heard the shots.

One, two . . . three . . . four—five—six. . . .

They sounded very near. They sounded almost as if they were inside him.

They acted like a signal of release on his overworked body. He fell flat on his face in the sand, and lay there panting and groaning.

He wanted to find out about the shots. He rolled over and tried to get up. But the pain wouldn't let him. It sat on his chest, an invisible conqueror, and sent needle probes of anguish and shame through his trembling limbs.

ELEVEN

HE LAY THERE until the edge of the pain had dulled, and his lungs no longer felt like a couple of ripped balloons. He lay there for perhaps five minutes, sick with anxiety, his mind cataloguing all the more lurid possibilities like a hysterical computer. Eventually, after about three or four minutes that stretched into dreadful hours, the various aches in his body were reduced to a scale on which they could be handled. He summoned the strength to get to his feet—a tricky operation—and began to hobble back towards the camp. . . . The leader of the expedition! He smiled cynically. A goddamned bloody marvellous leader of the expedition he'd made! He couldn't even lead a self-respecting troop of boy scouts. . . .

There was nobody at Camp One when Avery arrived. There was nothing but devastation. The tents, flapping drunkenly in the slight breeze, with half their ropes severed, seemed to gaze at him with mute reproach. The camping equipment was scattered crazily over quite a wide area. The trunks had been flung about, and so had their contents.

Avery found his paints and canvas boards half buried in the sand. Many of the packets of cigarettes had been opened, crushed and tossed carelessly aside. Several of the L.P. records had been wantonly smashed, but strangely enough the record player itself had survived.

Mary's sweets lay scattered with various items of clothing and underwear, suggesting, ludicrously, the combined remains of a rather violent and extravagant children's party and a communal sex-orgy. Barbara's possessions reeked of whisky—several of her bottles had been smashed apparently just for the hell of it. But the biggest surprise of all came from the widely distributed contents of Tom's trunk.

Avery remembered how only the night before—already it seemed a year ago—Tom had been so coyly secretive about his possessions. Well, the secret—or secrets—was out now; and so was the reason for Tom's reticence. The torn and tattered remnants of his fantasy world lay grotesquely and garishly on the sand—dozens of photographs and colour prints of pin-up girls. Some evidently taken from magazines and some rather too revealing to be acquired by other than 'private subscription'. There they lay in various states of dress, undress, provocation, invitation and so on. Among them were even snaps of one or two naked and bored-looking couples engaging in the sexual act in various and somewhat improbable postures.

Somehow, in this place and in this situation, the total impression was not of pornography exposed but of a cruel and tragic illusion. Poor Tom! Here were the symbols of his loneliness, his personal hell, his private despair.

Before he did anything else at all, before he even thought of anything else, Avery was moved to gather up the pathetic scraps of card and paper and try to get them back into Tom's trunk, as if they had never been disturbed. It was not decent in the true sense of the word that a man's weakness should be exposed and consequently mocked in such a fashion.

Even as he gathered them up, Avery knew that his hope of concealing what had happened was a futile one. And what the hell did it matter, anyway? Quite possibly Tom was dead by now, if the destruction here was anything to go by. Quite possibly the girls were dead as well and he, Avery, was wasting valuable time and effort for a stupid bloody reason when he ought to be concentrating entirely upon problems of personal security and survival. But he went on collecting the sad survivors of Tom's pornographic collection just the same.

He was so intent on his task that he did not even hear Mary and Barbara return. They found him among the wreckage of the camp, scrabbling about on his knees, picking up the soiled, two-dimensional scraps of a scattered dream world.

Mary began to laugh. There was a taut note of hysteria in her voice.

'Shut up!' said Avery brutally. 'Nothing is funny any more. I lost my sense of humour a while back.'

He stood up and looked at them both. Their clothing was torn, their hands and arms were scratched. Mary was bleeding from a cut above her eye.

'What the hell have you two been doing—fighting off hordes of sex-starved Indians?' He hadn't meant to say that. He was so unutterably glad to see them alive and relatively unharmed that he had to say something harsh to stop himself from dancing for joy or flinging his arms wildly and possessively round them both. Suddenly, inexplicably, they were no longer just Mary and Barbara. They belonged to him, they were part of his family. They were wives, sisters, mothers, sweethearts—anything that would give an excuse for kinship. He knew that he loved them. He knew because he knew how much he had been afraid.

'Sorry if we interrupted your private study,' said Barbara acidly. She dropped the empty gun on the grass in front of one of the tents. 'We got chased up a small tree by one of those dear little rhinotype creatures. And then the cunning little devil decided to bulldoze the tree over.' She shuddered at the recollection. 'God, they die hard, those things do. I kept pumping bullets into its head until I swear it began to rattle. . . . But, as I say, if we'd known you were engaged in vital research, maybe we'd have just sacrificed ourselves with dignity.'

Suddenly, Avery smiled. 'I'm sorry. . . . I mean really sorry. . . . I—I was so glad to see you I could have cried.'

'Instead of which. . .' observed Barbara. She gazed pointedly at the photographs.

'Not mine,' he said, feeling irrationally like a traitor. 'I heard the shots, ran too far, and too fast, fell in a heap, then staggered back to find the remnants of our happy home. I thought. . . . Hell! I don't know what I thought.'

'If they aren't yours,' said Mary, 'then they must be—'

'Christ! There's not much choice, is there?' He exploded. 'And is that all you can worry about? You two nearly got killed, the camp has just about been flattened, God alone knows where Tom is—but your sensitive souls are shocked by a few pathetic little pin-ups. Where's your perspective?'

'It died with the rhinotype,' said Mary, suddenly fierce. 'But if these objects of art are so important that you have to collect them first, we'd better help.' She bent down and began to gather a few of the pictures.

'I was hoping to get them stowed away before Tom came back,' said Avery dully. 'It . . . It seemed the kindest thing to do. . . . You needn't bother now, Mary. He's coming along the beach. He must have heard the shots, too, I suppose.'

Tom was about a couple of hundred yards away when Avery saw him. He had the body of what looked like a miniature deer slung round his neck and shoulders. He walked jauntily, like a man who seemed reasonably well pleased with life. When he was about fifty yards away, he saw what had happened to the camp and came forward at a jog-trot. At twenty yards or so, he saw the three of them waiting for him, frozen as in a tableau. He saw also one or two of the pin-ups that had been caught by the wind. He dropped the body of the animal and came towards the group slowly. His face was expressionless, his eyes remote.

'Glad to see you in one piece,' said Avery with an attempt at lightness. 'It's been a day of catastrophes. The girls nearly got hammered by a homicidal rhinoceros. I heard the shots, started running and gave myself a sort of Grade A heart attack.'

Tom said nothing. He knelt down and began to collect the rest of the pictures.

Avery watched him. He didn't know what to say or do.

'It's all right, Tom,' Barbara spoke. Her voice

was gentle—too gentle. 'My weakness is whisky. Richard and Mary have weaknesses, too. These things don't matter any more.'

Tom said nothing. He went on collecting the pictures. Silence flapped among the four of them, a heavy curtain of tension.

After a moment or two, Mary laid a hand on his shoulder. 'Tom, dear, there's no need to be ashamed. . . .' She hesitated, then went on. 'I fill myself with sweets—compulsively—I just can't help it. . . .I have a rag doll and—and I have to sleep with it held tightly between my legs. . . .' She swallowed. 'Because if I don't, I'm afraid. And then I begin to shake all over.'

Mentally, Avery took off his non-existent hat to her. Mary was the quiet one, the timid one, the prudish one. But, by God, she was wonderful!

She went on: '*Please,* Tom. We're not sniggering. We might have done yesterday, or in London a week ago. But not now. Please don't be ashamed.'

'Ashamed!' Tom turned an agonized, tear-stained face up to her. His voice was high, almost shrill. 'Ashamed! Do you know what these amusing little pictures have robbed me of—fifteen years of manhood! And you tell me not to be ashamed.' He laughed and the laughter was cracked with anguish. 'An eminent Viennese gentleman of the psychiatric persuasion once claimed humorously that sex was merely an unsatisfactory substitute for masturbation. I, God help me, spent fifteen years proving the thesis for him. . . . I bet you don't even know what masturbation is. . . . My father knew. He was a parson. He used to tell us choir boys all about the evils of flesh the on alternate Sundays. Masturbation produced insanity, paralysis, every rotten disease you could think of.

. . . I believed him. I believed every single word he said—until one day I had no father and the village had no parson. Do you know why? Because he was doing eighteen months for sodomy. There was a kid—a little horror—but my father used to say he had a face like an angel's. He may have done—but, Jesus, he had a mind like a sewage farm. . . . And who corrupted who? Your guess is as good as mine. I've been wondering for fifteen years. . . . And I've played it safe. Oh, yes, by heaven I played it safe. I never had a woman. I never had anybody. I wasn't going to make the same mistake twice. I wasn't ever going to trust anybody again. . . . Well, what did it bring me? It brought me those dearly loved four-colour harlots in all shapes and sizes. It brought me nights of three-dimensional dreams, so strong I felt as if I were drowning in a black marble bath with the water at blood temperature. It brought me days of misery, days of penitence—and more empty synthetic nights of splendour. . . . It brought me a lifetime of retreat.'

Suddenly, he collapsed upon the ground and lay there sobbing.

TWELVE

IT WAS EVENING by the time they had restored some semblance of order to Camp One. It was evening, warm and clear; and the bright jewellery of the sky was dominated once more by a pair of palely glowing moons.

Avery, Mary and Barbara were sitting round the fire, recovering from the trauma of the day and digesting a meal of steak—cut from the side of Tom's Lilliputian deer—supplemented with fruit. Tom had had the luck to chase the deer into a thicket, where it became hopelessly entangled. He had been able to break its neck with a staff he had provided for himself.

He had not, however, enjoyed the spoils of the hunt. When, at last he had regained control of himself after the humiliating exposure of his private world, he joined the others in salvaging what was left of their possessions. But he said nothing, and moved about almost as if he were in a trance. Mary tried to shake him out of it, but her approaches were blocked by silence. After a time, she stopped trying.

At last the camp was in reasonable shape, and Tom spoke once more. He said in quite a normal voice: 'Barbara, I wonder if you would be so kind as to spare me half a bottle of whisky? I'm celebrating an extra birthday.'

She gave him a bottle and, clutching the photographs in one hand, he retired with it into the tent he and Avery shared. That was a couple of hours ago. He had not come out since. There had been no sound other than the occasional muffled movements of the bottle.

Avery stared moodily into the fire. Here endeth the second day, he thought. Here endeth also pride, self-confidence, organization and bloody leadership.

He had been a fool to think they could play The Famous Four on Coral Island in a situation like this. He had been a fool not to insist on maximum security all the time. He had, in fact, been a fool without any qualification whatsoever.

It must have been one or more of Mary's 'Greek Gods' who 'processed' the camp. Clearly it could not have been the work of animals. And unless, he, she, it or, more probably, they had attacked purely by chance when the camp was deserted, it seemed to follow in a nastily logical sort of way that he, she, it or, more probably, they had had Camp One under observation for quite a time. Even now, of course, they might still be crouching in the darkness about fifty yards away, planning the next little surprise entertainment. Avery shivered at the thought, and tried to will it out of his mind. If he continued in that vein, pretty soon he would have the darkness ringed entirely by unseen eyes—and a couple of battalions of homicidal savages.

Fortunately, Barbara diverted his thoughts to a more constructive level.

'What are we going to do?' she said simply.

He had an answer for that one. Anybody could

have an answer for that one. 'Move,' he said. 'As soon as it's daylight we are going to find a place that can easily be defended. Then we are going to protect ourselves as well as we can, and live in a state of semi-siege until further notice.' He could have added: or until we just disintegrate, or the bogyman gets us, or we fall ill, or the wild life takes care of us, or golden spheres come raining out of the fourth dimension, or we all get anaesthetized once more by crystals and wake up in wonderland. As things were, each of these seemed quite a reasonable possibility. In fact the only absurd notion was that the four of them had any chance at all of surviving for any length of time.

But Barbara, also, was lonely and afraid. And it was the alleged duty of an English gentleman (extinct species!), thought Avery, to put women and children first. So he decided to make up reassuring fairy tales.

'Don't worry too much. This is only the second day. We'll get on top of things before very long. . . . Today was a shambles all round, but in a way it was also a lucky break. It taught us that we don't take any damn single thing for granted. At all. That was a lesson worth knowing, and all it costs us was a few luxuries and a few bits of camping equipment. First thing tomorrow we'll look for a base that is pretty near impregnable, and then—'

'Lift up your hearts,' interrupted Barbara drily. 'It may have cost us more than you think, Richard.' She nodded her head towards the tent. 'And I know who paid the bill.'

Mary sighed. 'Poor Tom. . . . Do you think he'll be all right?'

'Of course, he'll be all right,' snapped Avery

irritably. 'He's taken a kick in the psyche, that's all. Everybody collects one sooner or later. Usually, it's sooner rather than later.'

'Evidently Tom has been collecting them with monotonous regularity for about fifteen years. Maybe this final one will operate on a make-or-break principle. . . . I wouldn't like to guess which.'

At that moment, the tent flap was pushed back. And Tom appeared. The whisky bottle was in his hand—empty.

'Children,' he said thickly, 'I do believe you are taking the name of one Thomas Sutton Esquire considerably in vain. . . . May I join the party?'

Avery thought nonchalance was the best approach. 'Glad you were able to come.'

'Would you like something to eat?' asked Mary. 'That steak was delicious.'

Tom shook his head vigorously. 'For he on honey dew hath fed, and drunk the milk of paradise. . . . Pardon me, folks, I have presents for you.' He disappeared into the tent and then emerged with an armful of pictures.

He gave one to Avery. 'Cop that one, old boy. *Coitus exoticus*. How the devil do they get into that position, eh?'

Avery committed himself to nonchalance irrevocably. 'There are two solutions. They either do it by plastic surgery or mirrors.'

Tom cackled. 'Not bad, skipper. Let's humour the poor devil, eh? Pretend nothing has happened, and all that rot. . . . The stiff upper lip, by God!'

He turned to Barbara, and thrust one of the pictures at her. 'Consider the artistic merits of this one, me proud beauty. *Coitus syntheticus*. The weapon, dear lady, is of finest teak.'

'Tom,' said Barbara evenly, 'what the hell are you trying to prove?'

He was delighted. 'Ah, a good question! I see that I have before me a mature and sensible audience tonight. What am I trying to prove? What, indeed! Dear lady, there is nothing left to prove. All is *fait accompli*. Tom, the infantile regressive has been unmasked. The late Thomas Sutton Esquire now stands before you, mewling and psychiatrically puking, as with his former wont.'

Mary began to cry. 'Tom, darling, stop it! Stop it! We need you. . . . We need you so much.' The words came half muffled by sobs. But their effect was magical.

'Methinks I hear a damsel in distress,' began Tom. Then he stopped, blinked, swayed perilously near to the fire and finally sat down by Mary's side. 'What did you say? Mary, what did you say?'

'Don't,' she sniffed, 'don't hurt yourself any more, please. . . . We can't manage without you. . . . You and Richard. . . . You have to keep us together.'

He put an arm round her shoulder. In a moment, he seemed miraculously sober. 'You said: Tom, darling. . . . That was nice—but unnecessary. It doesn't have to mean anything, Mary. You must understand that. It doesn't have to mean anything at all. . . . But that you can say: Tom, darling, after what you know. . . . Nobody ever said: Tom, darling, before. . . . My mother, I suppose. Nobody else. . . . Don't cry, Mary. I need to be needed. I've needed it a long time.'

Avery wanted to annihilate himself. So did Barbara. This was something too sharp, too searing and too private to be shared. But there was nothing to do, nowhere to go. They could only sit and watch.

Suddenly, Tom grabbed all the photographs and pinups and flung them on the fire. 'A burnt offering to the goddess of diminishing hormones,' he cried. 'The Englishman's farewell to obscenity.' He laughed and—further miracles—the laughter had a healthy ring about it. 'God, what a price those would have brought in the Lower Fourth!'

Mary dried her eyes. 'It's an example,' she said seriously. 'I'm going to swear off chocolates and my rag doll.'

Barbara began to giggle. 'Prigs,' she said. 'You're both so much stronger than I am. Can I lean on my whisky just a little longer?'

'This is the headquarters of the League of Purity, Madam,' said Tom. He hiccuped. 'You shall be rationed to three slugs a day—by order of Herr Kapitan Richard, who, being without vice, is the noblest of us all.'

Barbara smiled and glanced at Avery. 'He's not without vice, Tom. He has the worst one of all.'

Avery raised an eyebrow. 'And what is my particular vice?'

Barbara placed a hand on his knee. 'Remembering,' she said gently. 'Remembering far too much.'

He thought of Christine. And then he thought of the deadly coldness of all the years without her. Maybe Barbara was right. Maybe there was a kind of remembering that was itself a vice. Maybe it had to do with Pedestals and perfection—and the bitter, lonely happiness of creating an image that was too good to be true. He had tried to be honest—but what price honesty when you were looking for a convincing excuse for failure. Maybe Barbara was more right than she knew.

'So all God's chillun got vices,' he said lightly. 'Well, it looks as if we are going to have to translate a few of them into virtues—and the only worthwhile virtues in this particular dream world are the qualities that make for survival.'

THIRTEEN

THE NIGHT PASSED uneventfully. They took the watches in pairs—first Avery and Barbara, then Tom and Mary. There was a further innovation, unanticipated and by mutual consent. They went to sleep in pairs also. Not lovers, hardly as even as men and women. Almost as tired children, seeking the inexplicable comfort of huddling close together.

It was Tom and Mary who created the precedent. Avery had told them they could have about three hours before it became their turn for duty.

'Pity,' Tom had said, looking at Mary. 'We were just getting to know each other. . . . Well, I suppose it will keep till tomorrow.'

'It doesn't have to,' said Mary, surprisingly. 'One good thing about all this is that none of us has to conform to silly standards any more.'

Tom smiled and held out his hand. 'Only let there be honour among thieves. . . . Ready, Mary?'

'Yes, Tom.'

They went into what had formerly been 'the men's dorm'; and for a little while their subdued voices could be heard. Then there was silence.

Avery saw that Barbara was crying quietly. Or not crying, perhaps, but just letting tears flow down her cheek.

'Now what's wrong?'

'Nothing is wrong, Richard.' Her voice was quite calm. 'It's just that I think we are suddenly starting to be people. We weren't people until today. We were all trying to give puffed up performances—and all the time we were hamming our lines. . . . Now I think we are trying to find ourselves—and each other. In one way, it's a bit frightening. But it's good. It really is good.'

'I know what you mean,' said Avery. 'A few hours ago, Tom wanted to crawl into a deep hole, and we were all being superior. . . . It's odd how things change. . . . I'm beginning to think that whoever wrecked the camp today did us one hell of a service.'

Barbara shivered. 'One is enough. I just hope they don't try to do us any more good turns.'

When the time came for the second watch, Barbara and Avery went to sleep together with complete lack of self-consciousness. There was no disturbing surge of passion, only thankfulness and an odd sensation of relief. They might have been sharing the same bed for years.

Tom did not waken them until breakfast was ready. Breakfast consisted of fruit, water and what Tom enthusiastically described as venison-bacon, grilled on sticks, delicious and satisfying. Breakfast was taken shortly after dawn. It was going to be a long and busy day.

'Leader of the expedition,' said Tom, 'permission to speak.'

'Granted,' said Avery with a grin. 'But just remember that my term of office expires today. In view of my record, I doubt that I shall seek reelection.'

'Going off further at this unoriginal tangent,'

remarked Tom, 'somebody has to be the whipping boy when things go wrong. Myself, I don't much care for the privilege. It's far more satisfying to be able to blame everything on dear old Richard. I hereby propose your re-election for a further and indefinite term of office.'

'Seconded,' said Barbara.

'Carried,' laughed Mary.

'My one satisfaction,' said Avery, 'is that you will all live to regret it. . . . Now, Tom, what's on your mind?'

'Life insurance. I want to sell you a policy. When I was out hunting yesterday, I spotted the absolutely perfect natural fort. It's on the beach about half a mile away. A damn big lump of rock about ten feet high, almost circular, and it's even got grass on top. I know. I climbed it to have a look.'

Avery was interested. 'About how wide?'

Tom shrugged. 'Hard to say, really. Maybe twenty-five feet. There's only one snag as far as I can see.'

'What's that?'

'No water.'

'That's a big snag. You didn't prospect for any?'

'Didn't have time. I was too busy doing an imitation of a pointer.'

'Well, we shall have to take a look, that's all. One thing is sure, we'd be idiots to try to stay here. . . . Oh, and while I'm thinking about it—edicts. Nobody, but nobody goes anywhere alone from now on. We either operate in pairs or as a group.' He turned to Mary and Barbara. 'And while Tom and I inspect Castle Perilous, you two stay put. Keep the gun loaded and ready. If you get worried about anything, fire two shots in rapid succession. If any

Greek Gods try to fraternize, let them have it dead centre—unless there are more than four. In which case, surrender with all possible grace and think nice thoughts. . . . That's about all, I think.'

'It's enough,' said Barbara grimly.

The two men departed. They each took a knife and a hatchet. As they walked along the shore, Avery had the disturbing and irrational feeling that he was crossing into enemy territory.

Tom's solid piece of life insurance was in the almost mathematical centre of a small bay. They reached it without seeing any living things at all—except for a couple of noisy sea-birds.

The piece of rock was just as he had described it. It lay a yard or two above the high-water line and about thirty yards from the trees. There was one point where it was fairly easy to climb, and even there the footholds were not very large.

'If we decided on this place,' said Tom, when they had scrambled to the top, 'we shall have to make a ladder.'

Avery felt the layer of sandy turf. It wasn't bad. It wasn't bad at all. The whole rock was rather like a very shallow saucer with a ragged lip all the way round. But it was well drained, because there was a slight slope to seawards; and countless rainfalls had worn a small channel through the rocky lip.

'This is perfect,' announced Avery. 'All we need now is a water supply.'

They climbed down and set about finding one. It took them the best part of an hour, and the nearest part of the stream was almost quarter of a mile away and about a hundred yards inland. Getting water was going to be a wearisome business; but the relative impregnability of the rock outweighed the disadvantages of such a remote water supply.

'We'll move,' said Avery finally. 'Unless we find anywhere better—and I very much doubt it—this can be the permanent base. We'll just have to organize an armed water-carrying patrol.'

'Jesus H.!' said Tom. 'I don't much fancy lugging those blasted trunks all this way. They'll have to be hauled to the top by ropes.'

It took them—all four of them—the rest of the day to move to Camp Two. Mary and Barbara made several journeys with the smaller items of equipment. They even managed to carry the tents between them—one at a time. But they were not much help with the trunks.

Meanwhile, Tom and Avery, manhandling the trunks foot by foot, developed mangificent blisters and exceedingly short tempers. The sun was setting by the time they hauled the last one to the top of the rock. There was no fire—nobody had had time to collect any wood—and there was nothing to eat, for the same reason. However, with considerable foresight, Avery had insisted on getting in a supply of water before the move had started. And at midday they had gorged themselves on portions of the 'deertype' before leaving its carcass to rot at Camp One.

So, though they were all hungry, they were not exactly starving. They had managed to erect one of the tents before darkness fell; and, as a chill evening breeze began to blow in from the sea, they all stumbled into it wearily and huddled together.

As Tom said: 'If any of Mary's strength-through-joy merchants want to play fun and games tonight, they're welcome—provided the bastards don't wake me up before they murder me.'

It expressed the general sentiments perfectly. Nobody had enough energy left to keep watch. But in spite of their fatigue, with the exception of Mary, who seemed to settle down quite well with Tom's arms around her, they passed a troubled night.

When morning came, they were all stiff and sore. It had begun to rain heavily a little before dawn; and within the tent the sound of the rain was magnified.

But at last it stopped. Avery went outside and saw that the sky was clearing rapidly and that the sun, a hazy and watery yellow, was already well above the horizon and had broken through the fleecy banks of cloud.

He breathed in deeply, and savoured the clean rich sweetness of the morning air. Suddenly, in spite of his hunger, in spite of his lack of sleep, he felt good.

For a moment, he had a sharp mental vision of London in the morning rush hour. The Underground and buses packed with victims for the City's concentration camps; the dull suburban eyes; the newspapers with crisis headlines of the latest antics of some overrated sex symbol of the silver screen; the idiotic pronouncement of politicians and sports columnists; the classrooms full of rebellious children; the anonymity of drowning alone in the great group frenzy that was life in a large city.

And, for a moment, with a feeling of shock he realized that he was glad not that he was away from London—at least, not that particularly—but that he had at last made contact with people. People like Barbara and Mary and Tom.

Then the feeling was swamped in nostalgia. And in his mind the zombies faded and the Underground was repopulated with interesting people;

the newspapers were filled with international goodwill messages; and even the schoolroom was attractive.

He recognized the idealization for what it was and brushed it away. Neither that nor the first vision had been real. The truth—if there was such a thing as the truth—must lie somewhere half-way between.

Meanwhile, the inescapable fact was that, so far as he was concerned, London itself was no longer a fact.

The facts were companions, isolation and danger.

The immediate project was survival.

He called Tom out of the tent and together they went to search for fruit for breakfast. As they climbed down the side of their rocky citadel, Avery took the skin off some of his blisters.

The flesh underneath was raw and moist and pink. It began to sting a little, but he was glad of the pain. He felt it was the kind of stimulus he needed.

FOURTEEN

BY THE END OF the morning, Camp Two was an organized and going concern. Three tents had been erected: the trunks, covered with the remaining tent, had been stacked two deep on the seaward side as a windbreak; and all the camping equipment, clothing and personal possessions that might have any immediate use had been stowed away in the spare tent.

Tom and Avery had gathered wood for a fire and had even found time to make a crude and shaky ladder, which proved to be only a very slight improvement on the one part of the rock face that could be climbed without much difficulty. However, they were rather proud of the ladder. It was the principle that mattered.

Tom also spent some time wandering up and down the beach, collecting smooth, roundish rocks between five and ten pounds in weight. These he dumped at the foot of the ladder; and when he had got about a couple of dozen he threw them up to Avery, who stacked them at regular intervals round the small citadel: ammunition in case of siege. There was going to be a warm reception if anyone tried to wreck their camp a second time.

That afternoon, leaving the gun with Mary and Barbara, the two men went hunting. They struck inland, but took care not to wander more than a couple of miles from camp. It was an irrational limitation because, at that distance, they had no means of knowing if all was well back at the rock; and at the same time it placed a futile restriction on the scope of the hunt.

However, neither of them wanted to venture farther. The memory of recent events was still too much with them. Probably, thought Avery, after a day or two they would regain confidence. But, despite the fact that they had left Mary and Barbara with a supply of rocks and the gun, and despite the fact that it would be difficult to storm the camp except by a determined group prepared to suffer casualties, they both become increasingly worried—but pointedly avoided mentioning Camp Two on the brief occasions when they found it necessary to talk.

It was partly this preoccupation that was responsible for the failure of the hunt. They saw several animals—chiefly at some distance and on patches of grassland—but their clumsy efforts at stalking drove the creatures away. Both Tom and Avery had become familiar enough with the reference cards to know the kind of animals for which they were looking and the kind which they hoped to avoid.

They found more of the latter. Tom trod on a snake which, fortunately, was more surprised than he was and slithered away with remarkable speed; and Avery almost walked into a basking rhinotype. According to the cards it was edible; but, recalling the experience of Barbara and Mary, Avery formed the opinion that it was going to take an awful lot of killing—hardly a job for light hatchets and knives.

They had back-tracked away from the rhinotype and circled round it, at a respectful distance.

Time wore on, and it began to look as if all the useful animals had made previous arrangements to be elsewhere. Presently, they struck a stream—probably the one that supplied them with water—and decided to follow it for a while in the hope that they might catch some unsuspecting creature drinking. But apparently none were thirsty—or, more possibly, thought Avery, they had fairly regular drinking habits, and the hunt was just badly timed.

The stream, however, led them to an attractive glade, in which it broadened out into a long deep pool, served by a ragged cascade of water falling perhaps twenty feet from a rocky shelf at the far end. The pool itself was about fifty yards long, but at no point was it wider than about fifteen yards.

Tom sat on a boulder and wiped the sweat from his forehead. The afternoon had turned close and heavy; and if terrestrial weather was anything to go by, it was quite likely there would be a thunderstorm before very long.

'Let's take a five-minute breather, and then push off home,' suggested Tom. 'We can pick up some fruit on the way back. The bloody animals are on strike today.'

Avery joined him on the boulder. 'As soon as we can, we must do some systematic exploring inland,' he said reflectively. 'It would be one hell of a joke if we were only a few miles from some kind of civilization.'

'Hilarious,' agreed Tom without humour. 'But somehow I don't think it was the policy of the nuts that brought us here to dump us near anything useful at all. . . . Christ! Get down quick!'

As he slid behind the boulder, Avery briefly followed Tom's startled gaze. At the far end of the glade, near the waterfall, a man and a woman had appeared. They were tall, golden-haired, naked—except for a very brief kind of metallic apron hanging from the man's waist, and a blue piece of fabric drawn between the women's legs and apparently attached fore and aft to a cord round her hips.

'Mary's Greek types,' whispered Tom, 'literally in the flesh. Maybe they're the very jokers who had fun with our camp. If so, I've a good mind to—'

'Later,' said Avery impatiently. 'Let's see what kind of people they are first.' He raised his head cautiously and gazed over the top of the boulder.

The strangers were magnificent specimens. Avery judged that they were both well over six foot tall. The woman's body was soft and feminine, but each of her movements suggested power. The man had the shoulders, narrow hips and careless grace of an athlete. Even at that distance both of them seemed to exude confidence—physical and spiritual. Or perhaps it amounted to something more than confidence, thought Avery, as he watched the way they carried themselves. Perhaps it was more akin to arrogance.

Tom was studying them also; and he, too, was impressed. Crouching behind their boulder, the two men felt disconcertingly like a couple of schoolboys spying on the private world of adults.

The strangers appeared to be chatting and laughing to each other, though any sound they made was drowned by the sound of the waterfall. The man was carrying what seemed to be three short javelins: the woman had what looked like a miniature cross-bow.

Evidently they considered the pool and the waterfall to be a very attractive discovery. After a moment or two, the woman laid her cross-bow down on a broad slab of rock and dived into the pool. The man sat down on the rock and watched. She splashed about and appeared to be trying to tempt her companion to join her. But he, clearly, was determined to stay on watch.

Suddenly, along the edge of the pool about ten yards away from the boulder that hid Avery and Tom, there was a muffled splash followed by a brief arrow formation of ripples that disappeared almost immediately.

'Hell, what was that?' asked Tom.

Avery had caught a glimpse and was still recovering from the shock. 'A crocodile—Mark One,' he said horasely. 'About four yards of it.'

We'd better do something. Maybe it likes goddesses for lunch.'

That was the natural impulse—to stand up and shout. To do something—anything that would get the girl out of the water. But the man at the other end of the glade looked a tough customer. Before anybody could get the concept of crocodile into his head, he might translate the message as warlike intentions; and however things turned out, it was quite possible that somebody might get hurt, or killed—especially if these were the people who had worked off their aggressive feelings on Camp One. It would be ironic, thought Avery, if a pitched battle started because they had tried to save somebody's life. He was caught in an agony of indecision.

'Christ, we can't do nothing!' exploded Tom.

But even as he spoke, the problem had been solved.

The man at the other end of the glade stood up on his slab of rock. He peered intently at the pool for a moment or two. Then he stooped, picked up one of the javelins and balanced it speculatively in his hand. He had seen the crocodile. Avery sighed with relief.

But the puzzling thing was that the stranger made no effort to call his companion to safety. He let her splash about and enjoy herself. Only when the crocodile was obviously a few yards away did she appear to notice its shadow. And the next puzzling thing was that, instead of making a panicky dash for the edge of the pool, she just looked at the man—who made a slight motion with his head—pointed towards the crocodile and calmly trod water, waiting.

She did not have to wait long. The man's arm swung back, then the javelin, released from the flash of his extended hand, sped through the air in a smooth arc. It pierced the surface of the water not more than two yards ahead of the woman. But a foot below the surface it clearly found a target, for it hung like the mast of a sinking ship for a moment, quivering. Then the crocodile rose almost bodily out of the water, its jaws transfixed by the terrible weapon.

But by that time a second javelin was on its way; and that one took the crocodile in its soft belly.

Calmly, the woman swam clear of its death throes, then turned to watch the spectacle. To Avery's incredulous eyes, she seemed to be enjoying it.

The crocodile took quite a long time to die.

When, at last, the body was still she swam back to it and with considerable effort tore out the javelins. Finally, she returned with them to the bank.

The man helped her out of the water; and together they stood laughing and talking for a while, and pointing to the floating body. For some reason completely beyond Avery's comprehension, they seemed to find it vastly amusing. Eventually they turned away from the pool and made as if to go back the way they had come.

'I've just about seen everything now,' breathed Tom in awe. 'Me Tarzan, you Jane. Who in the world would have thought it could be for real?'

'Depends which world you are thinking of,' said Avery drily. Then he added: 'This might be a golden opportunity to find out where those two live.'

'Golden, perhaps. Dangerous, certainly,' observed Tom. 'The way he handled the javelins fills me with respect. I should hate to be on the receiving end. . . . Not to put too fine a point upon it, you and I can hardly be considered silent trackers of the forest.'

'Maybe you're right. Besides, it might be a long haul, and we have been away from camp quite long enough.'

'What about the food problem?'

'We'll have to be temporary vegetarians once again.'

It took them the best part of an hour to collect enough fruit and find their way back to camp. The threatened thunderstorm did not materialize; and by the time they had returned to the seashore, the sun hung low in the sky. The air was still. A thin spiral of smoke rose from Camp Two. Somebody had obviously lit the fire. Somebody was obviously hoping to have something to roast. Somebody was going to be disappointed.

'Shall we tell them,' asked Tom as they approached the rock, 'about Tarzan and his mate?'

'Not unless we have to,' said Avery enigmatically. 'Well, blessed be the saints—look at that!'

Tom followed his gaze. 'A rock pool, So? The tide is out.'

'Look closer, my old one.' Avery knelt by the pool and gazed at the thick smooth stones that were not stones. He prodded one with his knife, and it attempted to scuttle away.

'Crabs!' exclaimed Tom joyously.

In a couple of minutes they had scooped out half a dozen.

'The problem is carrying them.'

'Problem solved,' said Tom. He took off his shirt. 'If the little devils puncture it, Mary can go all womanly and do some darning.'

Looking and feeling like a couple of beachcombers, they ascended the rickety ladder with their precious loads of food.

They did not mention the incident at the pool to Mary and Barbara. But after the evening meal, when they were all settled comfortably round the fire, the topic came into the conversation tangentially.

There had been a brief and relaxed silence, when they had each been staring into the patterns of the fire and thinking private thoughts. It was a pleasant time of the day, thought Avery. It was the time between action—or the need for action and decisions—and oblivion. It was itself a twilight world of semi-nirvana, when journeys could be taken without moving (one of these days he *would* prove that they were on an island: it was so, because he felt it was so), when speculation could take on the appearance of reality, and when memories, dulled by warmth and relaxation after a good meal, could be indulged in without pain. He was all set to treat himself to a succulent and leisurely dessert of memories when Mary broke the spell.

'Suppose,' she said suddenly, 'there were two sets of guinea-pigs.'

'If you are going to talk about guinea-pigs,' said Barbara, 'I'm going to indulge in a little whisky. Anybody else want some?'

'Me,' said Tom.

'And me,' said Avery surprisingly. 'A double. I'll pour my own water.'

Barbara raised an eyebrow, then disappeared briefly into the tent.

'You mentioned the subject of guinea-pigs,' pursued Avery. 'Two sets, I believe.'

'Us and them,' said Mary. 'I have a theory.'

'First define *them*.'

Barbara had returned with the whisky and plastic tumblers.

'The Golden people,' said Mary. 'Since I'm the only person who's seen one, I suppose I'm the only person who believes in them. But somebody must have wrecked Camp One, and I think they did.'

Tom was about to say something, but Avery silenced him. 'Tell us about the theory,' he said.

'Well, there isn't much,' went on Mary brightly. 'I just think there are two sets of guinea-pigs, and we're one set. Of course, there may be even more for all I know. Maybe we haven't come across them yet.'

'You think there is a kind of experiment in progress?'

'Don't be pedantic, Richard,' said Barbara. 'By this time we know there's a kind of experiment in progress. Even Tom forgot all about habeas corpus when he spotted two moons in the sky. After all, nobody is going to snatch us across the light-years—or whatever they are—just to give us a tropical rest cure. Besides, think of those bloody eleven-plus questions we had in solitary confinement.'

'All right, darling, you've made your point,' said Avery with a smile. 'The question is—'

'You called me darling!' said Barbara.

'I'm sorry. Slip of the tongue.'

She smiled. 'Also, a strategic error. Now I shall expect it at regular intervals.'

He grinned uneasily, and took a drink of whisky. 'I'll try to remember. . . . Now where the hell was I?'

'The question is,' prompted Tom.

'Ah, yes. The question is: what for?'

'To see how we live,' suggested Mary.

'Not good enough,' objected Tom. 'If bug-eyed monsters can hop around London without exciting too much general comment, they can bloody well study us in our natural habitat.'

'That's so,' said Avery. 'But they may not be interested in our natural habitat.'

'Where does that get us, then?'

'Here,' answered Barbara drily. ' 'Neath two tropical moons, and all that jazz.'

'Stress conditions,' said Avery seriously. 'That's where it gets us. They want to find out how we behave under stress conditions.'

'Possibly,' conceded Tom, 'but so far nobody has dropped by to check our pulse rates or ask us to fill in any questionnaires.'

'I'll come to that later,' retorted Avery. 'If Mary's notion is right—and there is no reason to think that it isn't—and if another group or groups have been dumped in our vicinity—and there's a bit of evidence to support that one—then the situation gets complicated. Maybe our invisible bug-eyed scientists want to give us a little healthy competition.'

Mary looked searchingly at Tom and Avery. 'You've been holding out on us,' she said at length. 'There's something you know—or that you've seen—that you haven't told us about.'

'That's so,' agreed Avery contritely. 'There's something else, too. It happened a little before the camp was wrecked—or possibly while the operation was in progress. I didn't want to cause any panic by telling you. But I'm steadily coming to the conclusion that that's a stupid attitude. We aren't going to get anywhere, I think, unless we all learn to share everything. And now seems to be a good time to begin. . . . All right, tell them about this afternoon, Tom.'

Tom told them, succinctly and graphically. When he had finished, there was a brief silence.

Barbara shivered a little and tossed some more wood on to the fire. Sparks like transient glow-worms danced jerkily up into the night air.

'I'm almost wishing you'd left us in blissful ignorance,' she said quietly. 'The way Tom describes it, I'm tempted to believe that those two have walked straight out of a super-race myth.'

'My point exactly,' said Tom. 'The more I think about it, the more sure I am that those jokers didn't come from Earth.'

'The mind simply boggles,' observed Mary

wearily. 'The more you try to sort things out, the more inscrutable the whole situation gets.'

'Of course,' said Avery. 'They may be indigenous.'

'In what?' asked Barbara.

'Indigenous. They may belong here. . . . In that case, if we are the intruders, what they did to our camp—if they did it—is at least understandable.'

'No,' objected Mary with a curious conviction. 'This planet is neutral territory. We have all been brought here—us and them, and anyone else there may be.'

'What makes you so sure?' Avery was intrigued.

Then, with typical feminine para-logic, Mary became vague. 'Because it fits better. There must be a sort of pattern—oh, I can't explain it—but something has to be worked out. . . . And the people who brought us here are watching the process through some kind of celestial keyhole. . . . That's what I feel. I don't know if it makes any sense.'

'It makes sense,' said Avery soberly. 'The kind of sense I don't much care for.'

Barbara turned to him. 'While we are on the subject of astounding disclosures, I believe you have a small contribution to make.'

Avery smiled. 'Mine's a real tall one.'

'They can't come any taller than the one we have just had.'

'Judge for yourself.' He described the glowing sphere to them, his reactions to it, and the way it had just disappeared with a sound as of breaking splinters of glass, and without leaving any trace of its presence on the sand. But he did not mention his earlier fleeting vision of a land mass across the sea. It did not seem now to have much relevance to their predicament.

'Stone me!' exploded Tom, when he had finished. 'The whole set-up is getting crazier and crazier. . . . You're sure it was real?'

'No, of course I'm not sure,' retorted Avery. 'Who can be sure of anything here? But I'd darn well swear to it.'

'Perhaps it was just a sort of balloon,' suggested Mary, 'with a camera or something inside.'

'Yes,' said Avery, 'a balloon with the surface temperature of molten metal, and one that just disappears—camera and all—with a snap, crackle, pop.'

For a time there was silence, with each of them retreating into lonely, frightening and absurd worlds of speculation. Profitless speculation, since the facts themselves were absurd; and therefore the degree of improbability of any possible explanation could only be measured against a background that was itself improbable.

Presently, Avery got tired of trying to solve the insoluble. He got up, went into the supplies tent and came out again with the portable record player and the first record he laid his hands on.

'Let's see if we can get any music out of this thing.'

'Was that yours?' asked Barbara. 'Back on Earth, I mean.'

'No, I had a king-size one. I was—am—very fond of music. . . . I expect our crystal-packing friends just wanted to keep me happy.' He gave her a thin smile.

Then he found the key of the record player and wound its motor up. Evidently the mechanical motor operated some kind of small generator as well as the turntable, because the sound was produced from a tiny loudspeaker.

He put the record on and set the pick-up carefully against its edge. It turned out to be a selection from *My Fair Lady*.

For a moment or two everyone listened as if they had never heard such music before.

Then the lyric and the voice of Julie Andrews bravely made their début on an alien world. *All I want is a room somewhere*. . . . The sound, indescribably sweet, the thought, subtly appropriate, hung like a small invisible cloud of magic between the security of the firelight and the brooding ring of darkness that surrounded it.

Suddenly, the tension was eased. And they all began to smile at the lovely ridiculous words. But their smiles were just a little too fixed. Looking at his companions, Avery saw firelight mirrored in the suspicious brightness of their eyes. Doubtless his own were just the same. . . .

He held a hand out to Barbara. She took it. Tom and Mary were already leaning close together, drawing comfort from each other.

All I want is a room somewhere. . . .

Avery sighed and surrendered himself to the echoes of a distant world. It was a wonderful and acutely painful luxury.

FIFTEEN

AFTER THOSE FIRST few hectic days there came a period of relative calmness, a time of adjustment—and rest. They needed it. They needed it badly. They only realized how much strain they had been under in retrospect, when they had time to develop a routine for the normal processes of living; when they found that they even had time to spare—time off from the struggle for survival.

The only really significant event that occurred on the day after the incident at the pool was that Tom and Avery, out hunting, found the home of a whole colony of rabbitypes. The creatures lived underground as does the terrestrial rabbit, but they could also swim and climb trees. Their colony had been established in the banks of the stream that was Camp Two's water supply. It was about half a mile inland; and for fifty yards or more, the ground was riddled with innumerable rabbitype holes. The animals were even less intelligent than their terrestrial counterparts. The two men soon found that the easiest way to catch them was to knock them out of the trees with stones. They could be stunned with quite small stones; and a smooth hunting formula was soon developed.

Instead of looking for rabbitypes on the ground,

they scanned the tree tops. When one was found containing what Tom began to call bobtail fruit, Avery would station himself by the trunk, and Tom—who had a better aim—would let fly at the creatures with pebbles he had gathered for the purpose on the sea-shore. If he missed or merely startled the rabbitype, it would invariably begin to climb down the tree. As it had to descend backwards, gripping the trunk with the short claws on all six feet, all Avery had to do was pick it off and kill it by swinging its head sharply against the tree. If Tom scored a hit, whoever was nearest to where it fell from the tree would dive on it before it had time to regain its senses.

With a meat supply so easily assured, the two men felt that they had solved one of the major problems of existence. If necessary, they could live quite well off rabbitypes and fruit for an indefinite period.

Although Avery was consumed with curiosity about the kind of world to which they had been brought, exploration was held in abeyance for a while. His original impatience was tempered by the growing conviction that their stay—if not actually permanent—was going to be quite a long one. Exploration could wait. It could wait until they had learned more about their immediate environment, until they had become more confident and efficient in the art of survival. Avery was particularly anxious to avoid any encounter with the 'golden people' until—well, until it was no longer avoidable. Sooner or later there would have to be a meeting; but as experience so far had done nothing to convince him that the outcome would be harmonious, he felt it would be wise to avoid a possible clash until he, Tom, Mary and Barbara had become a more efficient group and therefore a better potential fighting unit.

After a day or two, they fell into a routine that enabled them to do most of the necessary work in the mornings, thus leaving the afternoons and evenings free for relaxation or 'optional tasks'.

Perched as it was on top of a sort of rocky pill-box, Camp Two gave them a great feeling of security. However, they continued to maintain watches throughout the night. Although the camp would be hard to attack, it was certainly not impregnable; and they did not intend being taken by surprise. But instead of having a fixed rota and fixed times for the watches, they developed a fairly informal system. If someone wanted to go to bed early, he, she—or both—did so; and the other or others stayed up late and were then relieved by whoever had had the most sleep. Sometimes the men kept watches alone; but more often the watches were kept by pairs. It was more enjoyable, it made the time pass more quickly and there was less danger of the watch going to sleep.

Avery was fascinated by what he privately called the psychological mechanics of the group. They had started off as four complete strangers, yet within three days they had neatly divided themselves into two pairs. For, without doubt, he and Barbara now enjoyed a 'special relationship' just as Tom and Mary did. Special was, perhaps, an inadequate word. It was not love, but it was not without love—the kind of love that, like invention, was the child of necessity. In such a group as theirs, each depended upon and drew strength from the others; but there was a special kind of dependency that did not seem overtly to have much to do with sex, yet it could only exist between a man and a woman. It was not love and it was not marriage; but under the circumstances it was, possibly, a near relation of both love and marriage.

At times, during the first couple of weeks, he wondered whether Tom and Mary had actually made love. Sexual intercourse, coitus, copulation were the clinical terms—but, somehow, they could not quite fit the love-making that was possible between Tom and Mary. Looking at them in the mornings, Avery could detect no outward sign, no subtle change, to indicate that their intimacy had achieved what was obviously its ultimate and logical end. For the time being, he decided, their need was more spiritual than physical. They clung to each other because they were alone, because they had been abandoned on a strange world under an alien sky, because they were Babes in the Wood. . . .

Such, at least, were his own feelings in his relationship with Barbara. Sometimes, in the quiet of the night, he would feel her stir against him, would feel her pressing close, would know that she was awake and would sense the stirring of desire. Inevitably his own body would react, and he would become ashamed. He would become ashamed because he was in the thrall of ridiculous and Quixotic allegiances. He would become ashamed because he felt that the act of love would itself be an act of betrayal—of Christine. He was, he knew, thinking, feeling, reacting like the clean-cut, monosyllabic hero of romantic fiction.

The reality had died fifteen years ago, and fifteen years ago the myth had been born. Sick with grief, he had indulged in the masochism of fostering it. He had built Christine up into a legend. In death, she was more beautiful than in life. In death, her love grew stronger—more possessive. He had violated her in the worst of all possible ways, for he had turned her memory into his private sickness.

Intellectually, he knew all this; yet he could not let go. Intellectually, he knew that he had raised the memory of Christine to be a barrier between him and all normal, human relationships. And now he could not break the barrier down.

It was stupid because, in the sense of absolute loyalty, he had already betrayed Christine—if betrayal was the right word. He betrayed her when he held out a hand to Barbara. He betrayed her when, as Tom and Mary did, they began to exchange private smiles and gestures. He betrayed her every night that he and Barbara lay down together. What, then, did the final betrayal matter? Nothing but good could come of it, for surely Christine's ghost would be laid.

But still he could not bring himself to do what his and Barbara's body wanted. He knew—or thought he knew—that it would not mean more than he wanted it to mean for Barbara. She had already told him that she was by no means a virgin; and he had gathered that life in the hot-house world of television cameras and synthetic drama had produced the inevitable crop of synthetic romances and tailor-made passions. . . . But, hating himself, pitying Barbara and pleading with a non-dimensional Christine, he still could not make love.

Barbara made no complaint, she was patient, she was tender. At times she was even strangely maternal. And he hated himself all the more. He was perverse, and he knew that he was desperately trying to make a virtue out of perversity. . . .

The normal daily routine at Camp Two began shortly after dawn. Early morning, they had discovered, was one of the best times of the day. Usually, there was still a touch of coolness in the air, but the promise of growing heat lay behind it. Early morning, when the air was clear and still and the sea rolled gently like a flexible mirror, was a time that seemed to taste like wine. Whoever was last on watch would be preparing breakfast, and whoever had been resting would take the canvas bucket to the stream and get the morning supply of water.

Breakfast was a time for turning over plans and projects—mostly ambitious ones that would either never be fulfilled or not for a long time. They were going to build a boat, they were going to design furniture for the camp, some day they might even build a house. Breakfast was a time when fantasy and reality blended into a heady mixture with the wine-sharp air.

Afterwards—and there was no need to hurry, because there were no trains to catch, no offices, studios or classrooms to go to, no appointments to be kept—afterwards, the task formula was thrown into gear. 'Housework' for Mary and Barbara: tidying the tents, airing the sleeping bags, doing any washing or mending, dumping the refuse and so on. While these domestic chores were in progress, Avery and Tom would collect more wood for the evening fire and would then set off on a hunting, fishing or fruit-collecting expedition—or, as it frequently turned out, a combined operation. So far their fishing was confined to the stream—a matter of string and bent pins, which was not terribly successful, or tickling, at which Tom developed an effective technique. The fish they caught, never more than about two and a half pounds in weight, tasted rather like inferior salmon. There were plans for deep sea fishing—but that, of course, required a boat—and something more sophisticated than bent pins.

It was Tom who first put forward the idea of making extra weapons. The 'armoury' with which they had been supplied consisted of two hatchets, four knives and a gun. As Tom pointed out, none of them could be expected to be effective for ever—particularly the gun; there were only thirty-four rounds of ammunition left. And it was quite possible that, in time, the hatchets and some of the knives would be lost or broken. The idea was to develop alternatives while they still had a full complement, so that any future loss would not be a catastrophe.

The first type of weapon they tried to make was a javelin. They had a go at making several on the style of those used by the golden people. But the results could hardly be regarded as an unqualified success.

Hard, straight wood was fairly easy to find. They cut it with hatchets, shaped it with knives, smoothed it with pieces of coarse rock. They toughened the ends by charring them slightly in the fire. They even tried to make blades out of rock. But somehow they could not get the knack of javelins. The balance was wrong, or the points were not tough enough, or they could not devise a satisfactory way of binding a flinty spike of rock to the shaft. After a time they abandoned the javelin project.

Then Avery had a better idea. He and Tom were getting adept at using the hatchets in various unorthodox ways. Tom had even managed to kill a fairly small but disproportionately agressive 'ape/bear' by throwing the hatchet so that the blade buried itself in the unfortunate animal's neck. Partly because of this incident, it occurred to Avery that the manufacture of throwing hatchets might be a better solution to the problem of weapons than either persevering with javelins or attempting ambitious mechanisms like cross-bows.

His design was simple. It was planned round the best kind of stone they could find in reasonable supply on the beach. This was a heavy, grey, metallic rock which was fairly plentiful and which could be worked without too much difficulty. They chipped it into roughly rectangular shape, about three inches by six inches, and about an inch thick at its widest part. The handle of the hatchet was made of a sturdy piece of hardish wood split, dried, then bound tightly together with leather thongs, so that the two-edged hatchet head was set securely between the two halves of the handle and bound on either side. The thongs were of 'cured' rabbitype skin.

This type of weapon was even more successful than they had hoped. Later, Tom added a further refinement by sharpening the head end of the handle into a spike. After considerable practice, they even developed throwing techniques that enabled them to choose between a cutting impact or a piercing impact.

They made eight such tomahawks—a task which took more than a fortnight—then they taught Mary and Barbara how to use them. After that, they began to feel a little more optimistic about the outcome of any violent encounter with the golden people. Provided it did not take place in open country, the tomahawks could be every bit as lethal as javelins or cross-bows. But their effective range was not much more than about twenty-five yards.

When the routine tasks of the morning had been accomplished, when lunch had been eaten and the heat of the day was strong enough to discourage strenuous exertion, they settled down to relax—sometimes individually, sometimes jointly.

Short siestas came in fashion. They were usually followed by a swim in the sea. Avery and Tom had explored their little bay carefully. The water was shallow—never more than five feet deep—up to about forty yards from the shore, where the sandy ledge fell away sharply and there was really deep water. In order to remind themselves of the danger, they made a couple of wooden buoys, attached by spare tent rope to heavy stones on the sea-bed. It was all right provided the swimmers kept to the shore side of the buoys.

Apart from crabs, which were painful rather than dangerous, the only vicious type of marine life that seemed to venture into the bay was a beautiful, iridescent rainbow fish that looked completely harmless—but packed a considerable voltage in the long, slender antennae that grew from its head. Avery was the first person to encounter the fish. He chased it playfully, expecting it to dart away. It didn't. It turned and charged.

The shock almost paralysed him, but fortunately Barbara was near to help him ashore. After that, everyone gave the occasional rainbow fish that ventured into their territory plenty of room.

Since no one had swimming suits, they at first tried to improvise with underwear. It was more trouble than it was worth. Presently, they cast all inhibitions aside and began to swim naked. Presently, their bodies grew lean and muscular and brown. . . .

Mary was an obsessional diarist. Back on Earth she had been keeping diaries for more than ten years. The thoughtful and inscrutable *They* who had transported them to this place had not forgotten Mary's diaries, her most treasured possessions. Nor had *They* neglected to provide her with a new five-year diary.

Avery tried to read some significance into the fact that it was a five-year diary. But so was Mary's last one—which proved nothing.

However, when she was discovered bringing her diary up to date one afternoon, Mary was promptly elected camp historian. Her entries were now no longer merely a private record, they became the official records of the group.

The first entry read: *Somehow got myself tangled up in a mad sort of dream with three perfect strangers. Hope it ends soon. I'm terribly afraid.* She had made this entry on the evening of the first day.

But now they were no longer perfect strangers. The dream had become a reality, while Earth itself had receded into a dream stature. The fear remained, but it was smaller. And, too, it was offset by companionship, growing confidence and the subtle, tranquillizing magic of sky and land and sea. . . .

On Earth Barbara had been an avid reader of mystery novels. Her trunk contained about fifty assorted paperbacks—most of which she had read before in 'the other life', and all of which were by authors she liked. Now, she read them again and again—and so did the others—these stories of a fantastic world of cities, shops, theatres, restaurants, flats, country houses and impossible people.

The plots and the people no longer mattered. It was the background that they liked to read about. Unfortunately, in most of the stories there was so little of the kind of background they wanted. But imagination came to their rescue. If a restaurant in Soho was mentioned, each of them, in his or her own way, would re-create the set vividly, would joyfully invent the décor, furnishings, menu, the head waiter's name—even the private life of the restaurateur.

Eventually, this elaborate extension of fiction became a game which they played with each other, half jokingly, half seriously. Tom, who had been car-crazy, would give pronouncements on the kind of cars owned or used by the characters. Barbara would itemize their wardrobes, Mary would deliver expertise on their tastes in entertainment, Avery would develop their lives and actions far outside the terms of the novel.

They called it the Inquest Game. It was more than a game. It was a mechanism for creating transient realities out of permanent illusions. . . .

So time passed, and slowly they began to adjust to a totally new way of life. Time passed, and each in turn made startling discoveries:

Despair was giving way to exhilaration. . . .

Regret for things past was shrinking before the satisfaction of things achieved. . . .

And loneliness was receding like a morning mist. . . .

SIXTEEN

IT WAS ONE MORNING when Tom and Avery were theoretically on a hunting expedition inland—though, in fact, Camp Two was already well supplied with meat—that Tom raised a problem that had evidently been troubling him for some time. They were sitting on a fallen tree, taking a breather; and Avery was idly cutting a design on the haft of his favourite tomahawk.

'I hope, old man, that we know each other well enough by now for you not to take offence at anything I say,' began Tom.

Avery looked at him curiously. These days, Tom never said 'old man' unless he was particularly nervous.

'We also know each other well enough not to beat about the bush,' remarked Avery. 'What's the problem?'

'Impotence,' said Tom quickly.

'I beg your pardon.'

'I said impotence. . . . With Mary.'

'Oh, sorry. It didn't register for a moment.' Avery was thinking: Here, ladies and gentlemen we have the Garden of Eden—only neuroses are more plentiful than apples.

Tom was baffled by the ensuing silence. He had expected something more than a non-committal response.

'A further relevant matter,' he went on desperately, 'is whether you and Barbara have made love. . . . At least, I think it's relevant.'

'Possibly. But I'm afraid I'm going to disappoint you. We haven't. . . . Well, not in that sense.'

'Why not?' Tom was surprised. 'Don't you like her enough?'

'I like her a great deal,' snapped Avery. 'Maybe that's part of the reason. . . . You aren't the only nut case, you know.'

'You haven't made love to her?' echoed Tom stupidly. The knowledge seemed to shatter foundations on which he was trying to build.

'I haven't made love to her,' explained Avery, 'not because I can't, not because I don't want to, but because I've got a damn silly problem of loyalties. There was a girl called Christine, and she died a long time ago—but I got into the peculiar habit of not letting her die, if you see what I mean.'

'You'll have to get over it some time,' Tom pointed out. 'Otherwise you'll both go dotty. . . . Anyway, what do you do about the dear old demon sex?'

'I kiss Barbara good night,' said Avery angrily, 'and go to sleep thinking about Christine—and if I'm lucky, I wake up in the morning with the problem solved until next time. . . . Does that answer your question?'

Tom shrugged. 'Poor Barbara.'

'Poor Barbara, indeed.' Then he added brutally: 'But impotence was the original topic, I believe. Your impotence.'

'Let's forget the whole matter, old man,' said Tom distantly. 'I didn't know it was going to upset you.'

Suddenly, the tension drained out of Avery. He knew that he was being unreasonable and bloody-minded. He wanted to make amends.

'Sorry, Tom. Fat lot of help I am. . . . Any idea what causes the impotence, or is it all a damned annoying mystery?'

'I think it's tenderness,' said Tom with an almost comic expression. 'Tenderness—and a history of pornography.' It was the first reference he had made to his private collection for a long, long time.

Avery put a hand on his shoulder. 'You'll have to elaborate further, my old one. I'm in a complete fog.'

Tom took a deep breath. 'The trouble is, I think I'm in love with Mary.'

'Congratulations. No problem, then.'

'Don't be a bloody dunce,' exploded Tom. 'That is the problem. For donkey's years, love and sex have been in separate compartments. You see what I mean? Sex was sordid. Love was something you only read about. Sex was just bosomy bitches—preferably in two dimensions, where they couldn't do you a mischief—and love, well, I never really believed in it, I suppose. . . . ' He swallowed, and the sweat dripped off his forehead. The confession was costing him something. 'The trouble is, I have tenderness for Mary, I respect her—so how the hell can I do something like that to her. . . . I suppose it's a sort of conditioning,' he wound up lamely. 'Pavlov's dog, and all that.'

Avery's heart went out to Tom. He was pitting himself against the habits of half a lifetime.

'There's one other small point,' said Avery gently. 'How do you think Mary really feels about you?'

'Affectionate,' babbled Tom. 'Most affectionate. I think the poor misguided girl really likes me. Hell, maybe she even loves me. . . . She gives me so much.'

At this point, Avery was beginning to feel like an old, old man.

'This is a case of the blind attempting to lead the helpless,' he said at length. 'But here goes. . . . There are lots of feminine roles, Tom—child, virgin, harlot, sister, wife, mother. My guess is that women—most women—want to be a bit of everything. I think Mary does. Your trouble is that you think you ought only to cherish her. . . . God dammit, she must know by now that you cherish her. What she wants next is for you to use her.'

'But how?' asked Tom helplessly.

'Use her body, man. Forget she has a soul. Treat her like a paid prostitute.'

Tom's eyes widened. 'I—I couldn't do it.'

Avery smiled. 'There's a remedy for that—four shots of Barbara's whisky. Strictly medicinal. Three shots for you and one for Mary.'

'But—'

'But me no buts. . . . Tonight, I'm going to take Barbara for a long walk on the beach. When we come back, we'll take first watch. With a bit of luck and some thoughtful help, Nature will take care of the rest.'

'I couldn't do it,' said Tom. 'Not to Mary.'

'Man, you bloody well will do it,' snapped Avery. 'Otherwise, I shall have a heart-to-heart talk with Mary myself, and tell her all about your piddling little inhibitions.'

'Steady on, old man,' said Tom hotly. 'We're in danger of getting just a shade personal.'

Avery began to laugh. 'May I quote you,' he gloated. 'It's the saying of the week.'

Without a word, and muttering as much dignity as possible, Tom stood up and began to walk away. Neither of them spoke all the way back to camp. Lunch was a very strained meal indeed. The two women, looking at them, suspected a major quarrel.

That evening, however, as he had said, Avery took Barbara along the beach. The evening was so warm that they decided on a moonlight swim—still a novelty, when there were two moons to provide the light.

By the time they got back to the rock, Tom and Mary had retired. Barbara was surprised, because Avery had said nothing to her about the plot. In fact, he had said very little at all; and though she had tried to draw him on the assumed difference with Tom, his answers had been infuriatingly evasive.

Avery spotted two empty tumblers by the camp fire. He sniffed them with satisfaction.

'If you'd like to turn in, I'll take the first watch,' he said to Barbara.

She was suspicious. 'Something's going on. What the hell is it?'

'Nothing at all, my sweet. I'll take the first watch. You get some sleep.'

'Whatever we do, we do together,' she said, firmly. 'Something is happening. I want to know what.'

'You'll probably find out in the fullness of time

. . . . Well, let's go to bed anyway. Precautions can go to blazes for one night. The devil will look after his own.'

Yawning, but still mystified, Barbara raised no objection. It had been a long time since there had been any contact with the golden people. Presently, she and Avery went into their tent.

In the morning, a single glance at Mary was sufficient to tell both Barbara and Avery that something had indeed happened. She looked not conventionally radiant, as women are supposed to look on such occasions, but a little surprised, a little tired and vaguely smug.

Tom looked perplexed and obscurely proud.

Barbara, with her woman's intuition, soon discovered what it was all about; and Avery already knew.

As he surreptitiously inspected them both with—as he thought—a somewhat clinical detachment, he felt a sudden shaft of envy, and guilt.

He was conscious of a great and complicated irony. He looked at Barbara, and saw that she, too, was envious. Suddenly, he wanted to hold her in his arms. But he didn't. He pretended to notice nothing at all.

'Physician,' he murmured softly, 'physician, heal thyself.'

SEVENTEEN

ABOUT A WEEK after what Avery privately called Tom and Mary's Nuptial Flight, contact was made with one of the golden people—a woman. It seemed, in retrospect, a rather indecisive kind of contact; but at least it was a beginning. And, if nothing else, it should surely have demonstrated to the golden people that the occupants of Camp Two did not harbour any warlike intentions.

One afternoon Tom and Avery had wandered inland in search of a rather rare kind of fruit that had become a great favourite with all of them. It was an odd mixture of grapefruit and coconut—refreshing and satisfying. The 'milk' had a distinctly grapefruity flavour about it, and so did the 'nut' part, which was soft and rubbery and could be chewed as a kind of thirst-quenching chewing gum. Even the shell was useful, being hard but not brittle. When it was dried in the sun, it made an almost nonporous bowl, several of which had now been added to the crockery supply at Camp Two.

If the fruit was peculiar, the tree on which it grew was even more peculiar. It stood on stilts—or rather dozens of long tough whitened roots that rose quite high from the ground, then curved in to join the short tree trunk. From a distance, the tree itself gave the impression of standing neatly on top of an old-fashioned bird-cage—about eight feet high.

Inevitably, the fruit came to be called bird-cage fruit. So far, Avery and Tom had only discovered half a dozen bird-cage trees. Another mysterious thing about them was that the ripe fruit seemed to disappear far more rapidly than could be accounted for by the occasional raids made to replenish the larder at Camp Two. The two men assumed that the fruit itself was probably attractive to various animals; and they had even considered devising ways of protecting 'their' crop.

But it was not the animals—or, at least, not wholly the animals—that had been reducing the supply, as they discovered when they returned to raid the largest tree they had found so far, and which was farther inland than the rest. It stood on a small patch of grassland; and because it was not restricted by the competition of other trees, its bird-cage was much wider and the dome formed by the roots was more flattened.

Climbing the bird-cage trees was a difficult business because the roots, though strong, were thin and slippery. Sometimes a foot would slip between the 'bars' of the cage. Then the climber had to force the roots apart and ease it out by himself, get someone to help him, or, if he was alone, slither cautiously back down the dome and hope that the gap between the roots at ground level would be wide enough for the foot to be pulled free.

That was what had happened to the golden woman: her foot had been trapped. But she was unlucky. The roots at the base on the side of the tree where she had been climbing were almost as close together as, and certainly much thicker than, they were higher up.

Tom and Avery found her sitting helplessly on the ground, a small cross-bow near by and, a yard or two away, a home-made basket on its side with two or three birdcage fruit spilling out of it. Fortunately, they were quite a distance away when they spotted her. The woman's immediate reaction was to wriggle towards her cross-bow (which must have been quite painful), snatch it and fit one of the short arrows that hung from it in a small quiver.

'Down!' shouted Avery—just in time. He and Tom flattened themselves in the thick grass, and almost simultaneously an arrow whistled a foot or two above Avery's head.

'Homicidal bitch!' said Tom. 'Harm can come to a young boy like this. . . . What the hell is she doing?'

'She got her foot trapped in the roots.'

'Serve her bloody right. Let's leave her to stew. No doubt her boy friend will come looking for her if she doesn't get home in time for dessert.'

Avery shook his head. 'The opportunity is too good to miss. If we can help her, it might eventually register that we are friendly and harmless.'

'Speak for yourself,' said Tom, fingering his tomahawk lovingly. 'Judging by what they did to Camp One, I bet these people don't even have a word for friendship. . . . ' He laughed grimly. 'Anyway, you'd look bloody silly trying to help her with three arrows stuck in your tummy.'

'There's a solution to that one,' retorted Avery. 'We make her use up all her ammunition.' He raised himself on one knee, then immediately fell flat again. Another arrow whirred peevishly overhead.

Tom smiled. 'She'll catch on to it, then you'll get out of place and collect one.

Avery shook his head. 'Wriggle a bit farther away from me. It's your turn this time.'

Tom let out a profanity; but he crawled a few yards to the right, raised himself and flopped back quickly. Another arrow came.

Avery waited a moment or two, then offered himself as a brief target. He hit the ground quickly; but no arrow came. Tom then exposed himself once more, but again there was no arrow. 'What did I tell you? She's tumbled to it.'

'We'll see.' Avery raised his head cautiously above the top of the grass.

The woman had an arrow fitted and ready, but she did not release it. Cautiously, Avery got up to his knees. Then the arrow came. He was lucky. It fouled in a high clump of grass and went veering off course. He hit the ground, with his heart thumping madly.

Tom was vastly amused. 'There you are, old sport. Fraternization just isn't popular.'

But Avery was determined not to be beaten. 'I think she's only got one shot left.'

'You hope. Personally, I'm not taking any more chances. It isn't worth it.'

Avery waited for a minute or two, then very slowly raised his head to grass-top level. The woman was still sitting there with her foot trapped and her cross-bow ready. She and Avery stared intently at each other across a distance of some thirty or forty yards. He saw that her breast was heaving, and she didn't look any too happy. So far as he could see, she didn't have any more arrows—but that, of course, might be a simple trick.

'Don't shoot,' he called. 'We want to help you.' Even as he shouted to her he was conscious of the ridiculousness of hoping to communicate in English. But at least she might disentangle a bit of the sense from the sound.

She made no move, but continued to glare at him apprehensively. He decided to take a chance and stand up. But no sooner were his head and shoulders visible than he noticed a slight movement of her hand. He hurled himself to one side as the arrow came, rolled over once, then stood upright.

'Idiot!' shouted Tom, who was still flat.

But the woman did not have any more arrows left. She flung the cross-bow down and, with low moans of pain, tried feverishly to free her trapped foot.

Avery began to walk towards her. Seeing that his gloomy predictions were not fulfilled, Tom also stood up and advanced. When they were about ten yards away, the woman stopped her futile endeavours and sat waiting for them, her fists clenched, her eyes sullen and afraid.

Avery came up close to her, crouched down and smiled. He gestured towards her trapped foot and the thick roots. '*We,*' he said, pointing to Tom and himself, 'want . . . to . . . help . . . *you.*' He pointed at her, then at the foot.

She flinched, but appeared to understand. Keeping his movements slow so that she would not be alarmed, Avery leaned forward and put out his hands towards the roots. At that moment the woman unclenched one of her hands, and using her arm almost like a short spear, jabbed the extended and rigid fingers unerringly into his solar plexus. Avery gave a painful grunt, then writhed on the ground. Before Tom could stop her, the woman delivered a chopping blow with her forearm to Avery's exposed throat.

It was a long time since he felt such pain. There was a drumming in his ears, trying to breathe was itself an agony of frustration, and a woolly mist seemed briefly to be closing in on him from all sides. Through it, he saw Tom's silhouette—and a raised tomahawk.

'Bitch!' yelled Tom. 'Try the play-back for size.' The tomahawk came down with a dull thud.

Wincing, groaning, Avery forced himself to sit up. The woman's body lay almost touching him. 'Bloody clown!' he croaked. 'What did you kill her for?'

Tom shook his head. 'Being soft-hearted, I didn't give her the edge, only the flat,' he said drily. 'A spot of sleep treatment seemed to be indicated. . . . She made a real mess of you in no time at all.'

Avery massaged his throat gently. It felt as if he had just swallowed a number of sharp stones. He coughed experimentally, and the pain made him wince; but at least the ache in his stomach was fading. The golden woman certainly packed a hell of a punch.

He looked down at her. The long, luxurious golden hair was spread like a ragged fan over the grass. Her eyes were closed, but she seemed to be breathing normally. In repose, her face was beautiful but—somehow not human. He tried to define its non-human quality, and couldn't. Evidently, he decided, it was the sum of many of the little peculiarities that occur in ordinary human beings—but not all at the same time.

Her ears were well formed, but they did not have any lobes, and simply joined the side of the face in a smooth downward sweep; her nostrils were wide, almost negroid, but the top of her nose was faintly Grecian, without any bridge, her lips were full, but the mouth seemed small in proportion to the rest of her face; her chin was firm, perhaps a shade emphatic, and her cheek bones were large and finely moulded, transforming the line from cheek to chin into an odd but attractive parabola.

Her body, apart from the blue band of fabric stretched between her legs, was naked, golden and quite superb. Altogether, she was a magnificent specimen. Avery judged that she must be at least four inches taller than either him or Tom—and probably several pounds heavier. And she was tough, as he knew from personal experience.

'Big tits,' observed Tom crudely, 'just as in my late collection. It makes you think, doesn't it? Maybe these birds were the original inventors of pornography.'

'And maybe they don't even know what it means,' retorted Avery acidly. He stood up. 'I hope you haven't cracked her skull.'

Tom grinned. 'For Christ's sake don't start feeling sorry for the bitch. She was trying to kill us—remember? Besides, I only clocked her fairly lightly. Supertypes like that are bound to have super-hard skulls.'

'Well, we'd better make use of the anaesthetic and get her foot out while she's still under.'

Tom bent down to examine the trapped leg. 'She's made quite a mess of it,' he said with some satisfaction. 'Serves her right for being bloody superior.'

The skin round the ankle, where it was caught between the thick bird-cage roots was torn and bleeding. The leg itself had swollen considerably and had developed a purplish hue.

Avery said: 'What do we do? Chop our way through the roots?'

Tom shook his head. 'I don't think she'd like that. The vibrations wouldn't improve her at all. Besides the hatchet might glance off and take a piece out of her. These things are like spring steel. . . . No, we'd better try and lever her out.'

They tried using one of the tomahawk handles as a lever, but the bird-cage roots wouldn't move. Avery finally solved the problem by forcing one of the bird-cage fruit that the woman had already collected between the roots, about a yard above her ankle. Then, using it as a wedge, he hammered it slowly down towards the ankle, and forced the roots apart.

Tom just managed to ease her foot through the gap before the increase in pressure and the battering it had taken suddenly became too much for the bird-cage fruit. Its shell collapsed inwards, and the roots resumed their original position.

'Ah, the proverbial nick of time,' said Tom.

Avery began to feel the bones in her foot. He didn't know much about anatomy—especially alien anatomy—but nothing seemed to be broken. The woman stirred and groaned. She tried to sit up, and fell back.

'It's as well she stayed out for the operation,' said Avery. 'You did her a good turn. . . . I think.'

He put the foot down gently, then raised the woman's head. She opened her eyes, closed them again, then shuddered. She gave another moan. Avery felt the bump where Tom had hit her. It was not as bad as he had expected. The hair had cushioned the blow.

'Now she's O.K., we can push off,' said Tom.

'We can't leave her like this.'

'Hell, it's more than she deserves!'

The woman managed to raise herself so that she was half sitting, half leaning against Avery. She saw that her foot was free and gave a sigh of relief. She looked at Avery and treated him to a somewhat doubtful smile.

'Let's try to get her on her feet,' suggested Tom.

'All right, but demonstrate on me first. Then she won't get any odd ideas.'

Tom solemnly lifted Avery to his feet, then pointed at the woman and made the same motion. She nodded.

They lifted her with difficulty. When she tried to put some weight on her injured foot, she winced but did not cry out.

'She needs a stick to lean on,' said Avery.

'Maybe we ought to go the whole hog, make a stretcher and take her home,' retorted Tom with sarcasm. 'Let's leave her now. She's O.K. And you never know, the boy friend may turn up.'

'We've got to find something for her to lean on.'

In the end, Tom went off to cut a branch from a less difficult tree than the birdcage. While he was away, Avery got the woman to practice taking a few steps leaning upon him. By the time Tom returned, she was managing reasonably well.

Tom had found a very sturdy piece of wood. He even trimmed the top to make a handle. 'This should hold her up,' he said drily. 'It's guaranteed tested for half a ton.'

'I think she might make it home under her own steam now,' said Avery. 'She's got a lot of stamina.' He watched her hobbling experimentally with the aid of the staff.

Suddenly, Tom had an idea. 'If we follow her at a discreet distance, we'll find out where their camp is. It might come in rather useful.'

Avery considered the idea, then finally decided against it. 'If she finds out she's being followed, she'll either lead us away or try to get us into some sort of trap. And if she doesn't find out, she may still lead us too near her playmates for comfort. Their philosophy seems to be shoot first and ask questions afterwards.'

Tom shrugged. 'We shan't get another opportunity like this—but you're supposed to be the brains.' Suddenly, he lifted his tomahawk and brought it crashing down on the woman's crossbow. He kicked the wreckage away. 'That will teach her not to be anti-social. . . . Now, we might as well collect the doctor's fee.' He began to pick up the remaining bird-cage fruit. 'They aren't any use to her. She'll have enough of a problem getting herself back to base.'

By an elaborate system of signs, Avery indicated to the woman that he and Tom were about to depart and that she was free to make her way back to wherever she lived.

Finally, as an irrational afterthought, Avery pointed to himself and said: 'Richard.' Then he pointed to Tom and gave his name, too.

The woman seemed to comprehend. She touched herself, and said something that sounded like: 'Zleetri.' Her voice was hard, almost masculine.

Then, with a curiously shy smile, she placed two extended fingers on her forehead and briefly touched Avery's forehead with the same two fingers. She turned to Tom, glanced momentarily at the debris of her cross-bow, and again touched her forehead. But she did not attempt to repeat the gesture on his. Gripping the staff tightly, she began to hobble away. She did not look back.

'Exit golden girl,' observed Tom, 'slightly battered and with food for thought.' He picked up Avery's tomahawk and gave it to him. 'Here, don't forget the old life-preserver. I hope you feel better now we've done our good deed for the day. . . . Incidentally, I wouldn't bank on her undying gratitude, if I were you. Those kind of people strike me as having short memories and long prejudices. You can tell from the way they react that they think they're God's chosen.'

Avery was not in the mood for argument. 'I'm hungry,' he said.

'So am I. Let's push off back to camp. . . . I'll tell you another thing. When they hear about this, Mary and Barbara aren't going to give any awards for gallantry. We have just helped to restore a potential enemy to active service.'

But Tom was wrong about Mary and Barbara. Regardless of what might or might not happen in the future, they both felt that Avery and Tom had taken the only course possible for civilized people. Instinctively, they knew it was important to maintain the basic ethics of civilization. And instinctively, they knew that, in the end, all worthwhile ethics could be reduced to that ancient principle: Do unto others. . . .

That evening, there was a heated discussion on the incident—Barbara, Mary and Avery versus Tom. Eventually, Tom retired in a sulk.

His attitude puzzled Avery. Although he had not cared much for the idea of trying to help the golden woman—particularly since she had done her best to kill them both—he had certainly been of as much practical assistance as Avery, if not more. What made the matter even more puzzling was that Tom had been positively eager to help when, some time ago, the other woman (or perhaps it was the same one) had been in danger from the crocodile in the pool.

Avery wondered what had caused the change. Perhaps the incident at the pool was itself responsible. It had certainly shown both of them that the golden people were formidable specimens. Perhaps, then, logically, Tom's present attitude was the right one—especially if it ever came to a question of open conflict between the two groups.

For then another principle would come into operation—more ancient than any ethical precept ever devised. A principle commonly known as Survival of the Fittest. . . .

EIGHTEEN

FOR NO REASON that he could consciously appreciate, as time went by the desire to explore grew into an obsession with Avery. It started a few days after he and Tom had found the golden woman at 'their' bird-cage tree. Oddly—and inexplicably—at first he tried to ignore it. But as the days added themselves up into uneventful weeks, so the pressure grew, until it could be contained no longer. He wanted suddenly and impossibly to explore in all directions, to find out as much as he could about the world they were living on.

At night the two moons and the strange pattern of stars tantalized him. By day, he stared at the seaward horizon, or along the shore, or at the long green phalanxes of trees and bush as if he would force them to yield their secrets by sheer willpower.

There were plenty of ways in which he could rationalize the urge to explore. He told himself that he and Tom, Barbara and Mary were slowly sinking into an insidious and primitive lethargy, they were becoming too content with the simple (and infuriatingly satisfying) routines of existence. They had been thrust into a strange situation and they had adapted too readily. Camp Two represented security. Unless they made a conscious effort to extend their knowledge and their dominion, both would ultimately, inevitably, shrink. If they continued to exist in the same old way, they would get to know intimately the small area of territory in which they now operated. By contrast, the unknown tracts of land would be regarded as dangerous. In the end, they might even become tabu. . . .

There were many arguments for exploration—all of them good ones, some of them even dramatic ones. But they were still rationalizations. The plain fact, he told himself moodily, was that he was getting bored with the so-called idyllic life. He was still infected with all the restlessness and discontent of an allegedly civilized mind.

He did not say anything to the others. They seemed happy enough and contented enough with what they already had. In the few months that they had been thrown together, there had been enough excitement, danger and minor crises to make them feel thankful for what they had managed to achieve. And it was certainly no mean achievement for four strangers to mould themselves into a fairly harmonious group.

Because he was busy repressing the thoughts that had begun to dominate him, Avery became taciturn and took to indulging in long solitary strolls when the others were bathing or just spending a lazy afternoon on the seashore. He always went armed on these expeditions, but fear of wild animals and the golden people had diminished. He was no longer the same person whom *They* had picked up, ill and flabby, one cold and dismal afternoon in another world of space and time. He was lean, weathered, muscular—and, he thought complacently, a fairly reasonable kind of hunting/fishing machine. He had despatched many animals that would formerly have sent him running; and had even wounded then ultimately finished off a small rhinotype by getting it groggy from a distance, then rushing in to tomahawk its head to a bloody pulp. Even Tom had not managed a rhinotype so far. Avery was proud of the distinction.

A solitary stroll, then, no longer seemed an abnormally hazardous venture. Being alone was a bitter-sweet pleasure for which his taste seemed to be growing.

Barbara was more aware of his inner turmoil than he suspected. She said little enough when he took himself off for long periods; but she charted the change in his moods and habits anxiously, trying vainly to persuade herself that his moodiness was an obscure variation on the theme of homesickness. They all suffered from it occasionally—but not nearly as much as they would have expected. There were times when they felt they would give anything to experience once again the sights and sounds of London. But the sensation would pass, and they would contrast the freedom of their new lives with the restrictions and frustrations of the old. And suddenly, the sunlight would seem brighter, and the sea utterly wonderful.

When she was not trying to cheat herself, Barbara knew that it was not homesickness that Avery was suffering from. And, in turn, she herself became subject to moods—fits of despondency, feelings of guilt and inadequacy.

There was a further complication to consider.

Recently, she and Avery had begun to make love. Or at least they began to have sexual intercourse. Avery, inspired by the altogether beneficial change in Tom and Mary, and at the same time feeling that he was denying Barbara something that was hers by hereditary right, had made tentative—and awkward—overtures in the darkness of their tent. Barbara had responded with enthusiasm—perhaps too much enthusiasm—for though the mechanics of the operation were perfect, it proved sadly to be no more than that: a mechanical operation. Physical passion received its quietus, for a time. The body was fulfilled, but the soul remained strangely empty.

They had made 'love' not more than half a dozen times. It, too, had become a formula. . . .

The storm broke one night when Avery felt impelled to 'do his duty' once again. He placed a hand on Barbara's breast—the same hand, the same breast—and slipped an arm round her shoulder, thoughtfully taking care, as usual, not to entangle it with her hair. Next would come the first kiss, a hard empty kiss, then a fondling and a stroking of her arms and neck; and then. . . .

Barbara could stand it no longer. She pushed him away. 'Not tonight—please. . . . '

He was surprised. 'Is anything wrong?' Even the gentleness of his voice was mechanical.

'Yes, there's a hell of a lot wrong,' she sobbed bitterly. 'Where are you? There's a part of you that's gone away, and I don't know where it is. I only know that it isn't here. . . . All that wants to make love to me is a body with a bloody, built-in, automatic, self-regulating social conscience.'

Her body shook with the intensity of her frustration. She hated Avery, she hated herself, she hated the words she had spoken; and, above all, she hated the treacherous, scalding tears.

Avery was appalled. 'Barbara. . . . Dear Barbara,' he said lamely. 'I'm so sorry.'

Having started the scene, and loathing herself for it, Barbara was determined to fight it out to a finish.

'What do you want?' she demanded angrily. 'What in God's name do you want? If you want me to act like a harlot, I'll do it. If you want me to pretend I'm a shy, cowering virgin, I'll do my best. I'll even crawl on all fours if it will make you happy. . . . But if I don't know what you want, how—how can I ever hope to give it?'

Avery felt like a swine. Hell, he told himself savagely, I *am* a bloody swine—with megalomaniac tendencies. . . .

'What I want,' he began, 'it's not what you can give me, Barbara.'

That made matters worse.

'Goddammit, what *do* you want?' she cried.

'I want to find out,' he said desperately. 'I want to find out what sort of world we've been dumped on, why we're here, what we can do about it. . . . I want to *know.* I want to know something more. . . .'

'Is that all?' She seemed to find it amusing. 'You're a liar! That's only a diversion! You want Christine's breast and Christine's lips. You don't want to find out anything at all. You just want to make love to a sad little ghost. . . . You're only looking for excuses.'

That was when he struck her. It was the first time he had ever hit a woman in anger. As soon as he had done it, he hoped—he hoped with all his heart—it would be the last.

'Tomorrow,' he said coldly, trying to hide his shame, 'tomorrow, I'm setting off to do a bit of exploration. I may be away two or three days. Perhaps by the time I get back—'

'You're not going alone,' she said savagely. 'That's a standing order—delivered by the illustrious leader of the expedition. I'm going with you. . . . Now hit me again, and try to change my mind.'

'Please yourself,' snapped Avery. 'I doubt whether I shall be much company.'

'When were you ever?' sighed Barbara. She felt empty. The anger had drained out of her. Only the frustration remained.

NINETEEN

THEY DID NOT start until late in the morning. Tom held no brief for what he called 'the exploring jaunt'. He voiced his objections loudly. What if they got lost? What if they ran into something they couldn't handle? What if the golden people found out they had gone and decided, in view of the reduced garrison, to attack Camp Two?

Avery met all his objections stolidly. They wouldn't get lost because they would stick to the coast. They wouldn't run into anything they couldn't handle, because they would take damn good care to avoid it. If the golden people had had it in mind to attack Camp Two, they could have found several perfectly good opportunities during the last few months; and anyway it was psychologically bad to let fear of attack dominate their lives all the time. It made for stagnation and withdrawal.

'I think you're a bloody nut case,' said Tom with heat. 'If you want to take risks, that's up to you—but why you have to drag Barbara off on this damnfool jaunt is completely beyond me.'

'I am not exactly dragging her with me,' retorted Avery drily. 'In fact, I'd be perfectly happy if she didn't come.'

'Well, I am coming, and that's an end of it,' snapped Barbara.

Tom looked at them both in bewilderment.

'How long do you think you'll be away?'

'Can't say. Perhaps three or four days.'

'Not good enough,' said Tom. 'You must fix a definite limit. If you aren't back by then, we'll assume the worst and plan accordingly.'

'In that case,' said Avery, with sarcasm, 'what would you propose to do?'

'That's our business,' said Tom shortly. 'But you can bet your boots we propose to stay alive.'

'I hardly expected you to harbour the death wish.'

'No. It's a damn good job it isn't infectious,' said Tom meaningly.

'We'll be back by the end of the fourth day, if that makes you feel any happier,' said Avery.

Strangely enough, Mary, the most timid one, was not against the venture. She was, in many respects, much wiser than Tom; and she sensed that there was a great deal more to Avery's obsession to find fresh woods and pastures new than was immediately apparent.

'Look after yourselves,' she said gently. 'Maybe Richard is right. Maybe we are sinking into a rut. . . . Anyway, it should be exciting. We'll have a party when you get back. It's the best excuse that's come up for a long time.' She kissed Barbara on the cheek, then turned to Avery. 'You'd better take special care of her, or I shall be really cross.'

'I'll do my best.'

Suddenly, Avery and Tom found themselves shaking hands.

'If you find any gold mines, send me a telegram,' said Tom.

Avery smiled. 'If *They* drop by with a bunch of return tickets to Earth, tell them we'll wait for the next ship.'

It was a hot morning. For some weeks it had seemed that the days were getting hotter and longer. Avery had formed a tentative theory that they had arrived on the planet in the winter season, and that it was now high summer. As he climbed down the ladder from Camp Two he was already sweating heavily. Maybe it would be a good idea to rest a little in the afternoon and save the main travelling spell until the relative cool of the evening.

His plan—if it could be dignified by such a name—was simply an extension of that one early and abortive attempt at exploration. He proposed to travel mainly along the coast—this time in the opposite direction—and, perhaps, on the way, make one or two sample probes inland. On the whole, travelling along the coast should be easier and faster than a long inland journey; and he also felt there would be less chance of being surprised by the golden people.

For obvious reasons, he and Barbara were travelling light. They took one of the large sleeping bags that *They* had provided, a couple of old whisky bottles that now did duty as water bottles, Avery's pocket gas lighter (for which *They* had even provided refills), a packet of cigarettes—though both of them only smoked rarely—a first-aid kit and the standard equipment of hunting knives and tomahawks.

Tom had wanted them to take the gun, but Avery

refused. He felt that since the garrison was being reduced, Camp Two should be left as secure as possible.

The ground they covered on the first morning, being nearer to camp, had already been gone over several times. It held no surprises. Avery, with the sleeping bag hanging in a neat roll over his shoulder, set a fast pace, as if he were impatient to get away from the known into the unknown. Barbara had difficulty keeping up with him. For the most part, they walked in silence.

After a couple of hours, they were both drenched in perspiration. The heat of the day had intensified, and even Avery felt that it would be far too tiring to attempt to walk through the afternoon.

They cut away from the shore and found a pleasant patch of grass, shaded by trees. While Barbara sank gratefully down on it, Avery went to collect fruit for lunch.

They slept and dozed almost till sundown. They did not lie in each other's arms. It was too hot for that and, besides, they were both still acutely conscious of what had happened the previous night.

The remainder of the fruit was finished off for the evening meal. They ate it as the sun, red and enormous, slipped smoothly over the edge of their world. The air had been still and heavy, but twilight brought an invigorating drift of coolness in from the sea. They went down to the shore, bathed their feet luxuriously and began to walk once more.

The coast rippled like a serpent. Sometimes, the shore disappeared and they had to find their way over small cliffs. Twice they had to wade across streams. But the going was not too difficult; and the twin moons, hanging in the sky like remote

Hallowe'en lanterns, cast an entrancing silver haze over the land and the sea.

Presently the air became unnaturally clear, and the sky was shot through with stars. From being depressed, Avery was suddenly exhilarated to a pitch of ecstasy. He felt he had never seen so many stars. They were like fire crystals lining the black velvet pocket of the universe: they were like glow-worms in a celestial forest.

The ecstasy intensified. He was no longer conscious of fatigue. He was hardly conscious of walking. And Barbara had ceased to exist.

At least, she ceased to exist until, after several hours, she said quietly: 'Sorry, Richard, I don't think I can go on any longer.'

He looked at her, surprised. Not surprised that she was tired, but surprised that she was actually there with him. They were on a smooth strip of sand that seemed to be absolutely and geometrically straight, stretching before and behind them until it was lost in the darkness.

At the sound of Barbara's voice, Avery felt oddly like a sleepwalker jerked out of his private dreamscape into a puzzling world of reality. He stood looking at her, almost without recognition. It was several seconds before he pulled himself together sufficiently to take in the meaning of what she had said.

'Well, there's no reason why we shouldn't sleep here just where we are,' he managed to say. He dropped the sleeping bag and began to unroll it.

Barbara started to undress. 'I'm going to bathe. Maybe it will take a bit of the weariness out of my limbs.'

Avery said nothing. He sat on the sleeping bag and lit a cigarette. He inhaled, and there was a burning sensation in his throat. The cigarettes had been kept too long. They wouldn't be fit for smoking much longer. Not that it mattered. He threw away the one he had just lit.

Barbara stood naked and stretched her arms luxuriously, revelling in the cool touch of the breeze.

Avery looked at her. She was all silver. Silver hair, silver shoulders, arms, breasts and body; slender silver legs. Only her face, half turned to the sea, was hidden in shadow.

He thought that he was seeing her—really *seeing* her—for the first time. Not the Barbara of Camp Two, not the ex-TV actress who used to need whisky, not even the patient creature with whom he had half-heartedly attempted to enter into the conspiracy of sex. But someone he had never known. A stranger, or perhaps a witch-girl. . . . Or just a woman. . . . Just Woman. . . .

The moment was hypnotic. It was only a moment, but it was hours. He was drowning in things he didn't understand. He was drowning in a whirlpool of life—his life. The pictures danced around him—around Barbara—crazy, kaleidoscopic. Fragments of the days when he could paint, fragments of his life with Christine, fragments of Christine herself—they all whirled about him like the torn pieces of a photograph. . . . Or like the contents of a museum razed by a hurricane. . . .

Only Barbara stood still, a living column of silver—the still centre of a darkly spinning world.

He wanted to paint again. He wanted to paint a stranger, a witch-girl, a woman. He wanted to paint in colours that could not exist. He wanted to make patterns that had never been seen before. He wanted to snatch unimaginable contours from many dimensions.

But the moment had ended. She turned and ran towards the sea.

'Barbara!' he called. But either she did not hear or she did not want to hear. The moment had gone.

He was left breathless, dazed, appalled. Barbara was already in the sea, a silver woman in a silver ocean.

Surely none of it—and the thought made him afraid—surely none of it could be real?

But it was real, disconcertingly real. Even painfully real. . . .

It was *too* real. He wanted to exorcize it.

He wanted to think of Christine, and couldn't. He wanted to see her, feel her near, listen to words frozen by time. He stared at the sky, but there were only the stars. He stared at the beach, but there was only the sand. The ghost—his only insurance against participating in all the lovely, unnerving pangs of life—the sweet, sad ghost would not come.

He stared at the water. For a splintering second, he could see nothing but the swell of a great liquid mirror. He was alone in the universe, because life had decided to wait for him no longer. Then suddenly Barbara's head broke the surface, and drops of water fell from it like dying stars. And he was no longer alone.

He wanted to call out to her, but the words would not come—not the right ones. Instead he began to tear feverishly at his clothes and shoes, hysterically afraid that he would lose something he had not even had time to know that he had found.

Avery ran down to the water, plunged in and began to swim towards her. She seemed to think it was some kind of game, for she dived away from him and was lost under the mirror. The water came up a little above his waist. He stood there uncertainly, wondering where she could be.

Barbara surfaced behind him. He spun round and gripped her shoulders. A look told her, even before he did. A strange look. An angry tenderness. . . .

'I love you!' he cried in a loud and surprised voice. 'I love you! I love you!' He felt like a blind man with the sudden, terrible gift of sight.

'Darling,' whispered Barbara. 'Oh, darling.' She clung to him with a great fierceness, as if there was much pain to be driven away by sheer pressure before they could hold each other gently and in peace.

Presently, he carried her back to the beach. It was not a time for words. They lay down and made love with more joy than passion.

Then they talked.

And presently, Barbara said: 'Darling. . . . Darling. . . . Love me again—please.'

And this time the passion was as great as the joy.

At first, they wanted tonight to have no ending. At first, they wanted to smash the invisible glass of time with a tremendous hammer blow of love. But then it came upon them—a discovery that seemed, itself, to be time-shattering—that love need not end with the night, that it could rise with the sun, blaze radiantly at noon, stir mysteriously and darkly with the shadows of evening.

They discovered, as for the first time, the impossible unending promise of tomorrow.

Presently, aching with all the pleasurable aches of passion, dazed and even joyously hurt with the sharpness of their love, they managed to get as far as the sleeping bag—and then shared and joined and finally demolished the two separate lonelinesses of their lives, in the short remaining hours of darkness.

TWENTY

AVERY AND BARBARA got back to Camp Two just before sunset on the third day. They came back from the opposite direction in which they had set out. Avery had proved his pet theory that they were living on an island.

But the trip had been a journey of exploration in more senses than one; for he and Barbara had found each other. After months of sharing the same predicament, the same uncertainties and achievements—and the same tent—they had become so familiar with each other that familiarity itself had become a barrier. Familiarity and the unseen presence of Christine.

Not that the memory of Christine was now dead. But it was no longer a private thing. It was a small, enclosed world that Avery at last wanted to share—a poignant fragment of history that belonged to Barbara as much as to him. It belonged now to Barbara because it belonged to her understanding of him. It had dominated his life, had helped to make him what he was; and because of that it would become part of their shared life also.

There was so much now to share, and they were hungry for sharing. They wanted to know about each other's childhood, each other's work, each other's ambitions. They wanted to capture the essence of all the separate years there had been before those curious crystals, lurking in a winter landscape, had started the sequence of events that brought them together on a world beyond the world's end.

For them, love had been a kind of explosion. They were suffering from a spiritual concussion; and they knew, happily, that it would be a long time before they could settle down to accept it calmly.

However, the shared delirium did not hinder them from carrying out Avery's original project. It merely turned it into a different kind of adventure—a double exploration.

That first morning they slept until the sun was well above the horizon; and, on waking, their first need was to make love again—perhaps to assure themselves that the discoveries of the night had not ended with the night.

It was a different kind of lovemaking. The physical desire was not so great. It was a lovemaking with much affection and much tenderness. They talked and even made fun of each other. Only at the climax, when they both seemed to be briefly lost inside a warm, bouncing ball of darkness, were they silent. Immediately afterwards, there was laughter and light.

'Darling, we shall have to stop this,' panted Avery. 'Otherwise we shall be crawling back to Camp Two on our knees and with our tails between our legs.'

'With your tail between my legs,' said Barbara impishly. 'I don't ever want to stop. Nobody told me it could be this nice. . . . Maybe that's because nobody knows.'

But they did manage to stop—by a great effort of willpower. Avery found some fruit, and they had breakfast—still naked, still unable to resist touching each other. Despite the fruit, they were very thirsty; but they did not find any drinking water until they had travelled two or three miles.

They marched conscientiously until after the sun had passed its zenith. Then they had another meal, and the heat of the afternoon provided an excuse for a siesta; and the siesta provided an excuse for more lovemaking.

They were bathed in sweat. Their sweat mingled. They gasped with the lovely, compulsive exertion; and the mingled scent of their bodies became an overwhelming aura; itself the most subtle of all aphrodisiacs.

As soon as the sun was touching the seaward horizon, they went down to the water and lay in the shallows for a while, hand in hand, recovering themselves. Then with the coming of twilight, they resumed the journey.

So far they had seen no trace of the golden people and very few animals—none of the dangerous ones. Perhaps it was, as Barbara had suggested, that, for once, a benevolent diety had carefully arranged matters for their benefit, as a form of compensation for past ordeals. They seemed to be truly alone in a world that had been specially created to allow men and women to discover each other.

As they walked at a very leisurely pace through the early evening. Avery began to have a mild and half-hearted attack of conscience. He felt, as he put it, that they really ought to have been 'a trifle more scientific' about the whole project.

'I thought we were being scientific,' said Barbara wickedly. 'We have just about tried every reasonable position that comes to mind.'

'Darling, you're sex-crazed. You know damn well what I mean. . . . We should have done about three miles on the coast, then a mile inland, then another three along the coast, and so on. . . . As it is, I don't even know how far we've come.'

'As it is,' retorted Barbara, 'I don't even care.'

But their carefree attitude nearly led them into trouble.

They had been strolling lazily along the coast for about four hours—with occasional rests—when they rounded a small headland. They were both being drawn into an almost hypnotic state by dancing patterns of moonlight on the sea; and so they did not notice the camp of the golden people until they were within fifty yards of it. If there had not been a fire to attract their attention, they might either have missed it altogether or walked straight into it.

Avery saw the fire a split second before Barbara. There was no need to tell her what to do. Half-crouching, they backtracked and then made for the cover of the nearby cliff. Its base was strewn with slabs of rock and large boulders. It was not a high cliff, and it did not seem difficult to climb. Avery had an idea.

'If we can get up there,' he whispered, pointing. 'We shall be able to look down on them and get a decent view.'

Barbara shivered. 'What if there's one of them sitting on top?'

'It's a risk,' he admitted, 'but not much of one. Not at this time of night. There's not much point in having a guard this far away from camp.'

They scrambled up the cliff face quite easily. It

was far from being vertical, and there were plenty of footholds. At the top they found that they had an almost clear view of the whole camp area, which was now about seventy feet below them and nearer, horizontally, than when they had first glimpsed it.

The golden people had found a different way of protecting themselves than building their camp on a rock. They had made a small clearing in a thickly wooded area. From the trees they had cut down, they had constructed two quite large hexagonal huts, complete with windows, doorways and porches. By the side of each hut there was a hemisphere whose smooth surface was almost dazzling in the moonlight. The hemispheres, thought Avery, were probably some kind of opaque glass or plastic. They appeared to be used as store-chambers. Standard equipment, perhaps—like cabin trunks. . . .

The two main huts were at a distance of about ten yards from each other. The fire was between them. On each side of it there were home-made benches and a table. The whole camp was surrounded by a moat, perhaps two yards wide. The water in it appeared to be flowing quite quickly. Avery could just make out what seemed to be a narrow supply channel disappearing into the trees and a small exit channel that took the surplus water down towards the beach. In the camp area on the shore side, he could discern a structure that looked like a portable bridge. Probably it was pushed across the moat every morning and withdrawn every evening.

Only one of the golden people, a man, was visible. He was sitting on one of the benches and appeared to be constructing something out of wood. But on the flimsy evidence of the two huts, and on a sort of vague principle of symmetry, Avery decided that altogether there must be a population of four. Goddammit, there had to be! *They*–the tantalizing, inscrutable *They*–had set up some kind of experiment involving two opposed groups.

Avery was filled with admiration for the golden people—and also with an intensely personal feeling of inadequacy. Assuming—as a reasonable hypothesis—that both groups had been set down on this planet at the same time, and again assuming that they, too, were strangers to each other and just ordinary representatives of their race, they had already achieved a hell of a lot. Not for them the easy existence. They had set about establishing a base that could later be expanded. They were builders, pioneers—not indolent, expatriated city types. . . .

Of course, there was still the possibility that they were indigenous. But the more Avery thought about it, the more improbable it seemed. No, they were not indigenous. They, too, were guinea-pigs in exile. But what guinea-pigs! Already they had diverted the course of a stream and made their own houses and furniture. Guinea pigs with a difference!

Avery hoped desperately that the kind of experiment *They* had devised was not the kind he suspected. But he began to feel that the hope was a forlorn one.

He wanted to stay and observe the camp a little longer, but Barbara was getting distinctly unhappy. 'Please, darling, let's get away from here now,' she whispered. 'The more I see of this place, the less I like it. These golden people give me the shudders.'

He squeezed her hand, and nodded. 'The bigger they come, the harder they fall,' he murmured lightly, but his voice lacked conviction.

They scrambled back down the cliff. Just as Avery had decided to make a wide detour inland, one of the moons was obscured by cloud. They took advantage of the brief and partial darkness to creep stealthily past the camp of the golden people, as close to the sea as possible.

The cloud was not as co-operative as they had hoped, and the moon emerged once more when they were almost parallel with the man on watch. He was no more than forty yards away, and if he had looked towards the shore he must surely have seen them. Avery gripped his tomahawk apprehensively, but the man was intent upon his work. After all, there was no need to keep a strict watch when your camp was protected by a six-foot moat!

With the camp safely behind them, Avery and Barbara kept up a brisk pace for the next couple of hours. They wanted to have as much distance as possible between them and the golden people when daylight came.

At last they were too tired to go any farther, and wearily unrolled the sleeping bag in a sandy hollow just above the high-water mark. They were too tired even to make love, and fell asleep very quickly. Dawn came far too soon.

They were still tired, but not *too* tired. And somehow—quite strangely separate from the physical aspect—they needed it. The love came quick and fierce and curiously refreshing. Afterwards, they bathed in the sea. Breakfast hung from a tree and was theirs for the reaching. . . .

'This, I'm afraid, is the point where we have to decide,' said Avery reluctantly.

'Decide what, darling?' Barbara used the word 'darling' on every possible occasion. It was still a luxury. It gave her much pleasure.

'Whether to play fair with Tom and Mary, and turn back—I promised we'd not be longer than four days—or whether to be damned selfish, take a chance and press on.'

Barbara sighed. The exploration did not matter to her all that much. But it mattered to Avery, therefore it mattered. . . .

'Actually,' she said at last, 'we've only really been away one and a half days. If you are so keen, we could keep going for nearly another day—but then we'd have to come back at a cracking pace and walk through most of the afternoons.' She sighed. 'I don't suppose there would be any time for love.'

'When we get back, we'll have all the time in the world for love.'

She smiled. 'It still won't be enough.'

They—or, rather, Avery—finally decided to take the gamble and continue going forward. As Barbara had said, they could afford the best part of another day; and then, if they found nothing worth finding, they would head back for camp at top speed. Provided they could get safely past the camp of the golden people a second time, the extra day would cost nothing more than two pairs of sore feet.

But as it happened, the gamble paid off. By lunch time they had reached a stretch of coast that suddenly and inexplicably seemed familiar to

Avery. There were no outstanding features—it was pretty much the same as the miles of coastline they had already passed—yet still there was something he associated with it. His bewilderment lasted for a few minutes, then suddenly he remembered.

'This is where I saw the metal sphere,' he told Barbara exultantly. 'A few miles farther on, there's a rock pool where I found some footprints . . . . God, it seems ages ago. . . . ' He grinned happily at her. 'We're only a couple of hours from Camp Two, sweetheart. . . . So it's an island, after all.'

You're sure this is the place?' she asked doubtfully. 'How can you recognize it?'

'I don't know—but I *do* recognize it. . . . Don't worry, I'm not suffering from delusions.'

Suddenly, Barbara was jubilant. 'Then if we're so near, there's no need to worry. We can have a glorious afternoon without any problems and still get back a day ahead of schedule. We could even—'

'No we can't.' He knew what she was thinking. 'Tom and Mary have probably been worrying their heads off. We ought to get back this evening.'

Barbara accepted defeat gracefully. 'Now we know what it's like,' she said, 'we can fix ourselves up with an official holiday later—and no record marches.'

Avery laughed. 'We can have a dozen a year if you feel like it—without any loss of pay.'

'But this will still be the most precious one,' she said. 'The honeymoon isn't over yet. Let's make the most of it.'

They did—all through the long hot afternoon. Then they bathed once more in the sea, and finally made their way back to camp, tired out, and with the deliciously shared guilt of intimate conspirators. As they passed the remembered rock pool, Avery thought about his fleeting vision of a land mass across the sea. He scanned the horizon intently; but, although the air was very clear, there was nothing to be seen. Perhaps it had been a bank of cloud after all. In his present mood, it did not seem to matter greatly. It was much more important that Barbara's hand was lying in his. . . .

Tom and Mary looked at their faces and instinctively understood. Mary had seen them coming, and all four met on the shore. They flung their arms round each other as if they had been separated for months.

'Well, now,' said Tom solemnly, 'you two look as if you have had a harrowing time—very harrowing indeed. I can see we shall have to nurse you back to health.'

'Only back to strength,' retorted Avery. 'We have already demonstrated the quality of our health. . . . Incidentally we've also found where the golden people live. And we *are* on an island, Tom, not a very big one. How the devil we managed to avoid finding out for so long, I'll never know.'

'We have news for you, too,' said Tom. 'Mary's pregnant. She suspected it for some time, but now she has the classic symptom.' He grinned. 'It operates early in the morning, just before breakfast—so that I have to do the work.'

'Felicitations,' said Avery to Mary. He kissed her. 'I only hope you don't get strange yearnings for pickled onions and that sort of thing. The nearest grocery shop is an awful long way.'

Barbara was feeling smug. 'If I don't join you at

the clinic soon, Mary dear, the law of averages will have gone bust.'

Suddenly, Tom became serious. 'Damned if I know what we are going to do about doctors and midwives and all that rot.'

But Mary was strangely unperturbed. 'Stop worrying. What do you think women have been doing for about a million years?'

As they were going back to camp, Avery had a sublime thought. 'We never drank that bottle of champagne, did we? I knew there would be a good excuse for it sooner or later.'

Tom began to hurry on ahead. 'I'll try to get it cooled down to blood temperature in the sea,' he called.

TWENTY-ONE

APART FROM MARY'S morning sickness—which, exasperatingly, sometimes became an afternoon sickness or an evening sickness—the next few days developed into a sort of halcyon period at Camp Two.

The first thing Avery did was draw a map of the island—although 'map' was far too grand a term for what was, essentially, a simple diagram based upon hazy recollections and measurements that were little more than imaginative guesswork. However, his calculations of the length of the Grand Tour, about forty-five miles, was derived from time spent actually on the move. It seemed reasonably sound, give or take a few miles.

That, then, was the perimeter of the island. He thought, though he could not be sure, that its outline was roughly that of a Chianti bottle. On the first day and part of the second he had the impression that, allowing for local irregularities, the coast tended to curve gently in one direction only. Then it appeared to go reasonably straight until it twisted quite sharply at the Chianti bottle's neck. By coast, he estimated that the camp of the golden people was about twenty miles away. But if his idea of the island's shape was right, both camps were roughly opposite each other—on the wide part of the bulge. Overland, the distance from Camp Two to that of the golden people should be about eight or ten miles.

'Now that we know roughly how near they live,' said Tom, 'I begin to feel a little less secure. Something tells me we are going to have real trouble on our hands, sooner or later.'

'Possibly,' said Avery. 'But life has been reasonably peaceful so far—apart from that little frolic of theirs in Camp One. Maybe they, too, have enough sense not to press their luck. If we had found out earlier where they were, and retaliated, the cold war would have been a pretty hot one by now.'

'I'd like to take a good look at their camp, all the same,' remarked Tom. 'You never know, we might learn something useful.'

Avery shook his head. 'There's too much risk of provoking them. Barbara and I were lucky. Next time—if there is a next time—the luck may run out. Eventually we'll try to find some way of establishing friendly contact; but it's the sort of thing that's best done slowly—very slowly.'

And that was how the matter was left for the time being. However, spurred on by what the golden people had achieved, Tom and Avery began to think very seriously of building some sort of permanent accommodation. In the cold light of day, Mary's pregnancy presented many problems. There was no serious obstacle to bringing up a baby in a tent; but it seemed, somehow, incongruous. Besides, on the assumption—which, as time passed, was growing into a certainty—that *They* did not intend to provide return tickets to Earth, it was clear that Camp Two could not be regarded as a suitable base forever. A more spacious settlement would be needed; for as Tom said—only half jokingly—if they were going to found a tribe, they ought to choose a good strip of land with *lebensraum*.

The weather seemed to be getting steadily hotter. Mary was the one to suffer most. The heat and the morning sickness sapped her energy, and she became listless. But fortunately, about ten days after Barbara and Avery had returned, rain came—not just a downpour, but a miniature monsoon. It lasted over a week, and during that time the air began to grow cooler and fresher. Apart from necessary excursions for food and water, they spent most of the time in their tents, reading, listening to the record player or making love.

Barbara was quite delighted about the monsoon because it meant that she and Avery were thrust into close proximity most of the time, and there was still so much of him that she wanted to discover, still so many things to be shared. The only real drawback to the monsoon was that it made cooking impossible; and although there was a great variety of fruit that they could eat, after a time they began to long for meat and fish.

The rain ended suddenly at dawn one morning. They came out of their tents to find a steaming and iridescent world. . . .

,Avery began to paint. He began to paint like a man possessed—or like one who was suddenly trying to recover all the wasted years.

The paints and canvas boards had lain in his trunk for months, untouched, unwanted. But now he was suddenly and profoundly grateful for them.

He was grateful that *They* should have provided them. Above all, he was simply grateful for being alive.

Now that the fever of painting was on him once more, he could think of hardly anything else—except Barbara. Hunting, fishing, collecting fruit, looking for a site for *the* camp—even swimming—all these had become annoying irrelevancies. They irritated him. The real things in life were problems of form and texture and composition. He began to look with new eyes at the alien world in which he found himself. He began to see it as if for the first time. What painter in the whole history of art had ever had such a glorious opportunity! As he worked, Avery decided that he was a very lucky man indeed.

He painted anything and everything. He painted landscapes and seascapes. He painted Camp Two and a still-life with fruit, rabbitype skins and tomahawks. He painted Tom and Mary swimming, and a nude and a head of Barbara. He even painted crabs in a rock pool.

After a time, Tom, who was getting more than a little impatient with Avery's obsession, took to going off on hunting or fruit collecting expeditions by himself. Sometimes, when she was well enough, he took Mary: sometimes, when she could be distracted from her admiration of the greatest painter since Leonardo, he took Barbara.

It was one of these hunting expeditions that brought the halcyon period to an end.

Avery had begun a portrait of Mary—which was to be, he announced, a birthday present to her son. . . . Or daughter. . . . Mary's sickness was slowly diminishing, but mornings were still an uneasy time for her. She was lethargic, and strenuous activity tended to produce unwelcome responses in her stomach. So mornings were an excellent opportunity to sit for the portrait. She felt she ought to be working; but Avery's contention that sitting was working helped to reduce her feelings of guilt at seeing Barbara do all the chores.

On this particular morning, however, she and Avery were alone in camp. The meat supply was down to zero, and so, almost, was the fruit supply. Tom and Barbara had gone to remedy the situation. They had not taken the gun because it was a standing rule that it should be kept at Camp Two for purely defensive purposes.

Time passed—with Avery quite oblivious of its passing—and Mary became tired of the sitting. They abandoned it for a spell, while Avery went to freshen up in the sea and Mary lay on the shore, relaxing and watching him. Presently, he came out.

'How about another short session before lunch? Or will it be too tiring?'

She nodded. 'I'm fine now, thanks. But it will only have to be a short one, because Tom and Barbara will be coming back any time.'

'Nonsense. They only left about an hour ago.'

She laughed. 'Tom's right. This painting mania has done a mischief to your faculties. . . . They have been away about three hours.'

Avery said nothing. He was already back at his painting. He had just seen something spontaneous in her eyes that he might otherwise have missed completely.

Presently, he saw that she was fidgeting. 'Do be still, dear—otherwise your left breast is going to look like a dented melon.'

'Sorry. . . . My back has been aching a bit.'

He was solicitous. 'Hell, you should have said

so as soon as it started. . . . No, it's not your fault, it's mine for being too bloody obsessional. Tom will murder me if he finds I've made you tired. . . . Shall I rub it a bit for you?'

She shook her head. 'I wish they'd get back. They've been away ages. Do you think anything can have happened?'

'Certainly not,' said Avery confidently. 'Tom can take care of most things. So can Barbara, too, for that matter.'

Mary stretched, then lay back on the sand. 'It's not most things I'm worried about,' she retorted.

Avery continued to add a few touches to the portrait. Presently he said: 'I've just thought of a name for our island. It ought to have a name. How about *El Dorado*?'

Mary smiled. 'Apart from golden spheres and golden people, it somehow doesn't seem like the sort of place where there is any real gold.'

He put down his brushes and stared critically at the portrait. Then he turned to her. 'If you'll excuse a hoary old platitude, my dear, the real gold is always only where you find it. . . . Somehow, my resentment of *Them* is growing less and less—because you and Tom, Barbara and I all seem to have found something that may or may not be gold, but if it isn't, by the Lord, it seems a darn good substitute. Personally, I'm happier now, I think, than I have ever been. . . . Yes, *El Dorado* sounds all right. Let's go democratic and take a vote on it when they get back.'

Mary sat up, looking anxiously along the shore and then at the luxuriant green wall of trees and vegetation. 'I wish they'd hurry up. I'm beginning to get worried. Something *must* have happened.'

'Nonsense,' began Avery. 'It's your condition

that makes—' He stopped. The words froze.

About forty yards away, a figure had just emerged from among the trees. It was Tom. He swayed and reeled uncertainly—like a drunken man trying to find his way home. As he stumbled towards them, Avery saw that his tattered brown shirt was ominously red.

Mary gave a pathetic cry and jumped to her feet. Avery ran towards Tom.

He blinked at them both and screwed his eyes up as if trying to focus. 'Sorry, old man,' he mumbled thickly. 'Not much good. . . . The bastards got Barbara. I—I.'

Suddenly he crumpled. The broken shaft of a javelin was sticking out of his back—high, near the shoulder.

TWENTY-TWO

SOMEHOW, BETWEEN THEM, they got him up the ladder and into a tent. Avery laid him face down, gently, on one of the camp beds.

Mary was white-faced and trembling. But when she spoke, she made a tremendous effort to keep her voice normal. 'Can—can you take it out, Richard?'

'Yes,' he said, with more confidence than he felt. 'I'll get it out. . . . You'd better go for some water . . . .And, Mary—don't hurry. You understand?'

She nodded dumbly, and went out of the tent.

Avery knelt down. 'Tom, old son, can you hear me?'

Pushing urgently through all his pity and friendship for Tom was something more selfish, more agonizingly personal. Barbara, Barbara, he thought. Please be all right. Oh, my love, please be all right. . . .

'Tom, can you hear me?' Avery was shocked at the sudden harshness in his voice. He wanted to know. He had to know. He fought back a terrible impulse to lift Tom up and shake the truth out of him.

'Tom! For Christ's sake, wake up!'

But there was no response. Tom had managed to

stay conscious until he got back, and that was all.

Oh, God, don't let him die, pleaded Avery. I must know. I *must*!

Then suddenly the panic stopped, and an icy calmness came over him. Sweat ran down his face and into his mouth. It was cold and bitter. He looked at Tom—eighteen inches of javelin sticking out of his back, and the blood pulsing darkly through the dark patches on his shirt where it had already dried and cracked—he looked at Tom and was filled with shame.

'Sorry, old son,' he murmured gently. 'I can't go to pieces on you, can I?'

He bent down to examine the javelin, mumbling to himself as he did so. 'Number one, it's got to come out. Number two, there's only one bloody way to get it out. . . . Don't hold it against me, Tom. Whatever happens, don't hold it against me. I'm only a poor ignorant clod trying to do my best.'

He gave the javelin a cautious and tentative pull. Nothing happened. It must be embedded in bone or muscle—possibly both.

Then he tried a quick hard wrench. All that happened this time was that Tom's body lifted an inch or two from the bed. It plopped back heavily, forcing out of him a vague sound that was half groan and half grunt.

Sweet Christ, thought Avery, what the hell am I going to do? Whatever it was, it was going to have to be done in a hurry. Mary wasn't going to sit on her anguish for ever.

The answer was obvious and logical; and he didn't like it at all, for it seemed somehow to reduce Tom to the status of a lump of meat. But Avery could think of nothing else, so it had to be done.

He placed one foot in the small of Tom's back, took a grip on the javelin with both hands, and heaved.

It came out. And with it, it tore out of Tom a thin, high-pitched animal scream that was mercifully cut off by returning unconsciousness. Avery was afraid there was going to be a fountain of blood—a result of his clumsiness in tearing an artery or vein—but there wasn't. It just bubbled out in a sad, thin rivulet. The javelin fell to the ground out of Avery's shaking fingers.

Mary came back with water and bandages from a first-aid kit. The sight of her galvanized Avery into action. He ripped Tom's shirt back and exposed the area all round the wound. The hole was smaller than he would have thought. He began to bathe the blood away. It was coming out slower.

'Richard, how is he?' Her vo1ce was flat, carefully drained of emotion. It sounded like a child making the supreme effort of not crying.

Avery took a gamble. 'Lucky, I think.' He smiled at her. 'Nothing vital seems to be hit. He's a tough customer, is your Tom. But I don't imagine he'll be doing handsprings for a few days.'

She seemed relieved, but not much. 'I wish I could have helped. I feel so. . . .' Her voice trailed away.

'We've got to stop this damn bleeding,' said Avery. 'I'm going to squeeze a wad of cotton wool through in the Dettol, then pack it over the wound and bind it as tight as I can. . . . Unless you can think of anything better?'

She shook her head.

They cleaned the wound thoroughly and pressed a small mountain of cotton wool over it. Then, while Mary held the cotton wool in position,

Avery turned Tom over and got him up into a half-sitting position.

By the time Mary had cut the rest of his shirt away, the cotton wool was soaked through. They got a bigger wad—in fact the rest of the supply—and pressed that on. Then Avery began to put on the bandage, winding tightly under the armpits and then across the chest and back, as high as possible. The first bandage lasted about six full turns. They put four on altogether.

While Avery was struggling to pin the last one, Tom—surprisingly, even miraculously—returned to consciousness.

'My back's burning,' he mumbled. 'What's happening to my back? Who the hell—' He opened his eyes wide and gripped Avery's arm weakly. 'Richard, did you. . . .?'

'Yes, it's out. Take it easy. . . . The operation was hardly a text-book example, but the patient is still alive.'

'Darling,' said Mary. 'How do you feel?'

More miracles. Tom managed a sound that might charitably be interpreted as a laugh. 'How do I feel? 'That's a good one! I need some whisky. . . . Oh, my God! They got Barbara!' The remembering of it seemed to hit him physically.

'You said that before.' Avery tried to keep his voice normal. 'Don't play it for suspense a second time.'

Mary found a bottle of whisky and held it to Tom's lips. She tilted it too much. He coughed and spluttered, and the whisky ran down his chest. The cough made him contort with pain.

He controlled both the pain and the cough with an effort. 'We must have gone too near their bloody camp, I suppose. . . . No, I'll be honest, I wanted to see their territory. . . . Don't even know whether we got anywhere near it. We were following a stream, Barbara thought it might be the one they used. . . . Next thing you know, we practically walked into one of the big boys. He had javelins, we had tomahawks. . . . We stood staring at each other for a couple of seconds—mutual shock. Then he began to play with a javelin, and I yelled to Barbara to run for it. . . . The first one missed us both. I stopped to throw a tomahawk then started after her. . . .Next thing, I collected it in the back. I must have made a hell of a noise. Barbara turned round and came towards me. Then I passed out.'

He glanced longingly at the whisky bottle, and Mary gave him another drink. He took care not to cough this time. 'When I came round, there was nothing. Except that Barbara's tomahawks were lying in the grass.' He hesitated, and avoided Avery's gaze. 'It—it looked as if there had been a bit of a struggle.' Again he hesitated. 'The only blood there was seemed to be mine. . . . God, it was hurting me. It was hurting bad. . . . I thought . . . I thought the next best thing to dying was to—' He stopped, and suddenly began to cry. . . . 'Don't know how the hell I got back,' he blubbered. 'I just had to. . . . Say something, Richard, for Christ's sake, say something. . . . You ought to ram that goddamned javelin down my throat!'

The telling of it, the shame, the unhappiness were all too much for Tom. He was still conscious, but his head slumped forwards on to his chest. The tears ran down his face, dripped off the end of his chin and mingled with blood and whisky. The sobbing hurt him, but he couldn't stop. Avery laid him carefully back on the bed.

'Not your fault, Tom,' he said with difficulty.

'Something was bound to happen sooner or later . . . . It seems that people like them don't think or feel like people like us. . . . Whatever happens now, I suppose in the end it's going to have to be a fight to a finish.'

But Tom wasn't listening any more. Too much pain, too much sheer endurance and too much exhaustion had pushed him mercifully down into a pit of darkness.

Mary took Avery's hand and held it. It was cold and clammy. 'What can we do?' she asked helplessly. 'Oh, Richard, what can we do?'

Suddenly, he seemed to come out of a trance. 'I've got to find out about Barbara, if she's. . .' He left it unsaid.

TWENTY-THREE

AVERY HAD PERCHED himself on a thick branch just above the main fork in a fairly tall tree. He sat there, almost motionless, watching. He had been there for about half an hour. He was some fifty yards away from the camp of the golden people, which he could see through a convenient and roughly triangular gap in the tree's thick foliage. Soon it would be sunset. Soon he would have to act.

He was not the type of person for whom violence had any attraction. The thought of it normally made him sick with fear. But his sudden hatred for these people, who had so abruptly brought his small world of happiness tumbling, was strong enough to dominate his fear; and was strong enough also to transmute part of it into a lust for vengeance.

The day, having started so happily, had turned into a traumatic nightmare. The shock that had been injected into his nervous system was still acting as a stimulant. Later, no doubt, there would be depression and reaction; but for the time being, it had made him into a computer with muscles and purpose, a machine running on borrowed energy.

He had eaten nothing since breakfast, but he did

not feel either hungry or tired. Anxiety and hatred were food enough.

However, the compulsion to find out about Barbara had not impaired the mechanical logic that began to drive him almost like an automaton. Before he left Camp Two he had made sure that Tom was as comfortable as possible. He had also gone to the stream for a fresh supply of water—he had an idea that Mary was going to need a lot of water for her patient—and had collected as much fruit as he could carry on the way back. That at least ensured that she would not have to leave Tom unattended for quite a while. When he had satisfied himself that nothing more could be done at the camp, he had armed himself with two knives and two tomahawks and set off. He would have liked to take the gun, but then Mary would not have been able to defend the camp effectively.

The journey had taken much longer than he anticipated—nearly four hours. At first he tried to follow Tom's trail; but that proved a hopeless task. He was not trained to follow a blood spoor—or, indeed, a spoor of any kind—and soon abandoned the idea. It would be faster to travel in the general direction of the camp of the golden people and hope that he would strike the stream that supplied their water. Eventually, he came to a stream that seemed as if it might be the right one; but after he had followed it for a couple of hours, he saw that it joined the sea on an uninhabited piece of the coast. Fortunately, he recognized the strip of shore. There was an odd little rock formation that had attracted his attention when he and Barbara had walked round the island.

So now he knew where he was. The camp of the golden people lay about another six miles away.

He struck inland once more, then turned to travel roughly parallel with the coast. Presently, he found the right stream. His progress became slow and cautious. He did not intend being taken by surprise.

Having found the camp, he needed a vantage point from which to observe it. He thought of the cliff that he and Barbara had used; but it was too exposed. Finally, he decided upon a tree.

His vigil proved to be a considerable challenge to the computer that was operating inside his head. For he could see Barbara.

She was, apparently, unharmed. That at least was a relief. But her condition was such as made him want to charge in, tomahawks flying, in an attempt to free her by sheer strength and determination. He had enough determination but strength? The odds were four to one—or, counting Barbara, four to two. Four golden people versus two human beings. The computer gave its logical answer. He would have to wait. He would have to wait for darkness and surprise. He would have to employ more strategy than strength.

Meanwhile he could only look at Barbara and let the cold rage churn inside him. They had stripped her of all her clothes. They had tied a rope or a thong round one of her ankles and had made the other end fast to a large, heavy stone. She could walk, but she had to carry the stone with her. And she could not go far or move fast.

They were mocking her. She was the new plaything. From the way they were treating her, it was evident that they wanted to reduce her to something half-way between a servant and a pet. Occasionally, one of the men would grab her in passing and play some stupid little trick upon her. At first, she had struggled; but a box or two on the ears, bringing her to her knees and making her half senseless, had demonstrated the futility of struggling. She tried to endure their attentions with indifference. This did not please them greatly, so they had gone to greater lengths to obtain a reaction.

One of them held her while the other, using a brush and some kind of blue dye or paint had made a curious symbol rather like the Greek *omega* on each of her breasts and her belly. This seemed to amuse them; but the two women who were watching appeared less enthusiastic. One of them tried to stop the men, but was pushed roughly away.

At the evening meal—which was still in progress—the golden people sat at their table, but Barbara was made to crouch on the ground. One of the women gave her a bowl of water and a platter with some kind of food on it. But when the men noticed this, the platter was taken away. Occasionally, they threw her scraps from the table. Then, since she made no move to eat, one of the men flung a heavy bone from which he had been cutting meat. Barbara was knocked over by the impact. The burst of laughter that greeted this amusing incident drifted across the fading light to Avery as he waited in the tree, praying for darkness.

He tried not to think how Barbara was feeling. He tried to concentrate only on forming an effective plan. . . . A plan! He had already made and discarded about twenty.

One thing was sure, though, he would have to try to catch the golden people at maximum disadvantage. That meant waiting until some of them had retired for the night. He hoped that only one would remain on watch. Given the element of surprise, he felt he could cope with one of them: two—particularly if they were both men—was a very doubtful proposition.

As the sun went down, they piled more wood on their fire. And it was fire itself that gave Avery an idea. If, when they finally went to sleep, he could somehow get quickly across the moat and start a fire in the doorways of the huts, he would at least be able to imprison temporarily whoever was inside. . . .If the fire was big enough. . . . But first he had to get into the camp and then he had to deal with the guards.

While the plan was still only half-formed in his mind, Avery climbed quietly down the tree, retreated a hundred yards or so and then began to collect a large armful of dry grass and dead twigs before the light faded completely. As he worked, the scheme crystallized in his mind.

The moat itself was no real problem. At its widest it was, perhaps, three yards. In a running long jump, Avery felt sure he could cover three yards. Whether he could do it with an armful of grass and a couple of tomahawks was, perhaps, a shade more debatable. But he did not have any serious doubts. The anger he felt did not permit him to doubt.

So, if only one man was on watch, the drill would be to take a running leap across the moat, tomahawk the watcher, dip the armful of grass into the fire, dump it in the doorway of one of the huts, slip back to the side of the other hut, then tomahawk the occupant as he or she came out. After all that, he would be able to attend to Barbara. . . .

It was a nice simple formula, he thought cynically. All it needed was good timing, one hundred per cent luck—and the golden people helpfully reacting as per blueprint. But the computer inside him rejected the cynicism. It told him that the plan was elaborate enough. If he tried anything more elaborate, it would be sure to come unstuck.

When he had collected enough grass and twigs, he went through the material carefully to make sure that it was all really dry. Then he made his way to the edge of the stream that fed the moat, scooped up handfuls of mud and plastered it over his face and body. . . . The commando touch—as in all the best war films. He smiled grimly to himself. He smiled at the thought of ex-schoolmaster Richard Avery, on an alien planet, tackling four superbeings with an armful of straw and a couple of home-made tomahawks. And then rescuing the traditional damsel in distress.

A year ago, just one short year ago, never in his wildest dreams—but this situation was wilder than anybody's wildest dreams. It was itself a dream—in three dimensions, with natural colour and full stereophonic sound.

He finished the smear campaign, picked up his armful of incendiary material and made his way cautiously back towards the enemy camp. He did not climb the tree again. There was no need to. Under cover of darkness he circled round the moat a distance of about twenty yards, looking for the best place to jump. When he had found it, he retreated a little, checked that one of the tomahawks and both sheath knives were firmly in his belt, then settled down to wait. He sat cross-legged on the ground. Under his left arm was the bundle of grass and in his right hand was his favourite tomahawk. He might have to wait hours, he knew, but he did not want to put them down. Hunched in the darkness, with mud on his face and body, and a cold anger seething inside him, he felt like a weird malignant gnome. He tried to relax, and couldn't—which was irritating, because he felt that he was probably in for a long, long wait.

He could see Barbara, crouching close to the camp fire, obviously cold. There were only three of the golden people visible: two men and a woman. They were drinking something from a kind of pitcher. Avery hoped that, whatever it was, it was intoxicating. They certainly seemed to be getting more boisterous. Presently one of the men offered Barbara a drink. He did so with what seemed to be a polite gesture. She refused it. The other man laughed, grabbed her hair and forced her head back. He poured the drink down her throat. She collapsed spluttering and coughing. The sound brought the other woman out of one of the huts. She knelt beside Barbara and appeared to be trying to soothe her. Presently, she gave it up and joined the others. Barbara recovered herself, picked up the stone that was tied to her ankle and edged surreptitiously away from the men.

Avery gripped his tomahawk tightly. There were many accounts to be settled.

Time passed. It passed so slowly that Avery began to be horribly afraid that the golden people were intent upon having an all-night party—perhaps to celebrate their victorious encounter with the inferior race.

But at last one of the men and one of the women stood up, yawned and stretched, then retired to a hut. That left two. Avery began to pray that the remaining man would eventually turn in, while the woman took the first watch. Chivalry to hell! It would probably be easier to tomahawk the woman.

For a time, it looked as if they were going to keep watch together. But in the end, the woman went. That left the man—and Barbara. She crouched on the far side of the fire, watching him. Occasionally, the man stood up and took a walk round the camp area, peering vaguely into the outer darkness. Occasionally he addressed some unintelligible remark to her. On one of his tours he stopped by the part of the moat opposite Avery and peered intently into the darkness for a moment or two. Avery began to sweat. He was sure the man had seen him; but at thirty yards and with mud daubed all over him it was hardly possible. He was sitting in the shadow of a bush, and though the moons had already risen, the sky was cloudy.

At last the man turned away and went to Barbara. He pulled her to her feet, pointed to the symbols on her breasts and belly, said something, then laughed. Finally, he sat down and poured himself another drink.

His back was to Avery. And Avery felt that he had waited long enough. He got to his feet silently and indulged in a few small movements and flexions to get rid of the stiffness. Then he took a careful look at the moat and at the ground leading towards it. He prayed fervently that there were no nasty holes.

Finally, he hitched the bundle of grass and twigs more firmly under his arm, took a few paces back and launched into action.

Fortunately the approach to the moat was fairly flat. He was so intent upon gathering speed that he almost missed the line where the ground sloped sharply to the water. But he saw it just in time, and took a flying leap.

As he landed on the other side, the plan—the master plan—began to go wrong. The first thing that happened was that Barbara let out a half-stifled scream. Coming flying out of the darkness as he did, he must have looked briefly like a demon from hell.

As Barbara screamed, Avery came crashing into the camp area and the man half turned. The tomahawk blow that should have buried a couple of pounds of stone in his brain glanced off his head. But he toppled forwards nevertheless.

Avery did not wait to inspect the damage, nor did he give Barbara more than a glance. There was no time. He dipped one end of the bundle of grass and twigs into the fire, forced himself to wait until he saw the flames and heard them crackle as they took hold, then he ran to the hut where two of the golden people slept and dumped it in the doorway. There was a satisfactory spitting as the flames and billows of smoke leapt up. The effect was even better than he had hoped.

Meanwhile, Barbara had realized what was happening. She had begun to work frantically at the leather thong tying the stone to her ankle. It was at that point that Avery's plan went to pieces. Being so near to her at last after all the terrible uncertainty and waiting, instead of making sure of the man he had struck and then going to the other hut to tomahawk the woman as she came out, he could only think of helping Barbara. The computer inside him had finally lost the battle with glands and sentiment.

Avery ran to Barbara, knelt by her, whipped out

his knife and began sawing at the leather. So far, they had not exchanged a word. So far, the entire assault had hardly lasted ten seconds.

Barbara looked up. Her first words came in a half scream. 'Look out, Richard!'

Avery dropped the knife and dived to one side. The point of a javelin bit into the ground where he had been kneeling.

He came to his feet and snatched the tomahawk from his belt all in one motion. He was unaware that his teeth were bared and that he was growling like an animal. He was only aware of the tall, formidable being who faced him—a man with blood trickling down the side of his head. A man with anger and pain in his eyes and a javelin in his hand. He was no more than two paces away, and he was jabbing viciously.

The private computer tried to make a comeback. Get in close! it told Avery. Get in close, or you've had it!

The javelin came and he managed to slap it to one side. With an angry cry, he raised the tomahawk and charged. What happened next was totally unexpected and totally disastrous. Instead of attempting to ward off the blow or even dodge it, Avery's opponent simply doubled himself up.

The force of the charge could not be checked. As Avery went hurtling helpless over the arched back, he tried a slashing stroke with the tomahawk—and missed.

The golden man suddenly straightened up. The thrust lifted Avery—already in mid-flight—and somersaulted him high in the air. He landed flat on his back and momentarily blacked out. Then he saw the javelin poised above him. He saw it and, behind it, a face contorted with pain and anger.

The man raised the javelin slightly for the death stroke. But suddenly there was someone else. A woman. Not Barbara.

She shouted something. But the man did not seem to hear. The expression on his face resolved into a ghastly smile.

Avery suddenly recognized the woman. 'Zleetri!' He did not know why he called her name. There was no rational explanation.

As the javelin came thrusting down, she gripped it, pulling it to one side. She pulled too hard. The man who was holding it thrust too hard. The javelin twisted.

Its point took her in the pit of the stomach. With a low, bewildered cry, she sank to her knees. The man stared at her in amazement. He hardly appeared to realize what had happened.

The private computer clicked away, and Avery seized his chance. He sprang up, butting the golden man in the solar plexus with his head. Avery put all his weight into the blow and was rewarded by an agonized grunt. The man buckled. As his head came down, Avery helped him along with a two-fisted blow on the back of his thick neck. Before the massive body hit the ground, Avery followed it up with a forceful kick.

Then he flung himself on top of the prostrate man and began savagely battering his head on the ground as if he intended to continue the satisfying process until his strength gave out.

Barbara had to drag him off. All through those few terrible moments, she had been sawing feverishly at the tough leather thong. Finally she had cut herself free.

'Richard! Richard!' she screamed. 'We've got to get out! For God's sake!'

He looked at her uncomprehendingly. Then sanity came back. He gave the man's head a final battering and let it drop. The golden woman was lying in her own blood, moaning. Avery knew she had saved his life. He wanted to help her—but . . . But he could not afford to. For Barbara's sake, he could not afford to. . . .

'Zleetri,' he murmured softly. 'Zleetri.' On an impulse, remembering the incident at the birdcage tree, he touched her forehead. As he did so, he glanced at the now burning hut. Any moment, its occupants would come leaping through the flames.

He grabbed Barbara's hand. 'The moat! We've got to jump it. Take a hell of a run. It's easy.'

Barbara, naked and barefoot, hesitated only a moment. Then she ran and launched herself across the water. She mistimed it and hit the far bank with an agonizing thud, her feet dangling in the water. Avery, who crossed a second later, grabbed her arms as she began to slip down.

While he was pulling her out, he saw that the two occupants of the hut, roused from their sleep, had finally had sense enough to jump through the flames in the doorway. They came out scorched, bewildered and utterly dismayed by what they found.

Barbara seemed to be unconscious. But as he gathered her into his arms and struggled into the blessed darkness, Avery had the consoling thought that pursuit—if any—would hardly be immediate. For once, the golden people were in a situation that was as much as—if not more than—they could handle.

Avery staggered on with his burden at a jog-trot for about a couple of hundred yards. Then his strength gave out, and they both fell in a heap.

Barbara had only been winded. For a few seconds, they lay groaning and gulping in the cool air with their heads close together. Then Avery sat up and listened. He could hear nothing. Nothing but the breeze in the trees.

'Can you walk?' he croaked.

'I . . . I think so. It will have to be slow. They took my shoes.'

He stood up. 'Put an arm round my neck and lean on me. I'll carry you a bit more when I've pulled myself together. We've got to get as far away as we can. . . . Are you hurt?'

'I don't think so. Are you?'

'No. Come on. We'll nurse each other later.'

'Oh, darling,' said Barbara.

It was so wonderful to hear it. There was really nothing more to be said.

They hobbled along for a while, with Avery half supporting her. Presently, he carried her for a spell. Then they hobbled some more.

They seemed to have been struggling on for a long time—but Avery judged that they had not covered more than a couple of miles—when Barbara began to cry.

'What is it?'

'Sorry, Richard. . . . I don't think I can go any farther.'

'I'll carry you, then.'

'No, please. . . . I—I'm feeling all shaken up.'

'This is a hell of a time to be feeling all shaken up,' he said with sudden savagery. 'Walk, damn you! Or at least let me carry you. I'll be civilized tomorrow, but tonight it's a question of survival.'

She let him carry her, but the crying became a sobbing. Presently he put her down.

'What is it?' he demanded roughly. 'Goddammit, you must be hurt!'

'Oh, darling,' she moaned, 'I'm not hurt. At least, I hope I'm not hurt. . . . I wanted so much to tell you—but not like this. . . . It feels strange and—and . . . ' the sobbing stopped her.

'Sweetheart, what is it?' His voice was tender this time. 'We're all right now. We can stay here if you like. Somehow, I don't think they will come looking for us yet. They've got enough on their hands.'

'Oh, my dear one,' she said. 'I'm pregnant, and I'm afraid for the baby. . . .' She shuddered. 'It feels all wrong, as if something has happened.'

He held her in his arms. He held her and murmured tender, meaningless things.

'Don't be afraid, my love,' he whispered finally, though he, too, was now afraid. 'We'll rest here. And as soon as there is a glimmer of light, I'll take you home.'

The use of the word 'home' did not sound odd in his ears. Home was a place of love and security, a place of comfort and known smells and routines that had become rituals. Home was Camp Two and Tom and Mary. Home was a concept whose meaning he had only learned to understand on a strange planet light-years away from Earth. . . .

They did not sleep. Presently he told her how Tom had got back, and how he had pulled the javelin out. Then, to take their minds off their own troubles, they looked at the stars—now known and friendly stars—and divided them up into constellations and played at naming them. . . . And they thought of their child, and prayed simply that they would not lose it. . . .

They whispered to each other of many things,

but they did not talk about the golden people. With the first sign of light, they stretched their weary and aching limbs and stumbled on in the rough direction of Camp Two.

The feelings of unrest in Barbara's stomach had subsided. She began to feel happier. But when, in the early light, she saw the strange symbols that had been painted on her body, she was suddenly and violently sick.

TWENTY-FOUR

THEY DID NOT get back to Camp Two until a little after midday. Avery had given Barbara his mud-caked shirt. They had started on the last leg of the journey shortly before dawn; but they were stiff and weary and depressed, and the going was slow. Instead of making directly towards camp, they headed towards the sea. Barbara was obsessed with the thought of bathing. It meant more to her than washing off the paint with which she had been daubed: it meant a symbolic cleansing after her ordeal at the hands of the golden people. For Avery, it had a purely practical value. He was covered with the gritty remains of the mud. It was all over his face, arms, body—in the creases of his skin and even in his hair. It made him itch. He thought longingly of the cool sea water.

Presently, unaccountably, their spirits rose. They could even look at each other and laugh. The warm sunlight seemed to diminish their tiredness and gave them strength enough to rejoice in each other. They became alive once more and were glad they could still share the adventure of living.

They came to the sea at last, and it was bright with the gold of early morning. They tumbled into it joyously. This was a baptism to wash away all the terrors of the night.

It took Barbara a long time to get rid of the blue symbols on her body—and she did not manage it entirely. After a few minutes both her breasts and her stomach became sore with the rubbing. Eventually she had to stop. All that remained was a pale blue outline of the symbols and red, angry patches of soreness.

They dried themselves simply by walking along the shore until the sun and wind had done the job for them. Then Barbara put on the shirt once more and they trekked back to camp.

There was a pleasant surprise waiting for them. Tom had already become—as he himself described it—a walking and talking case. His body, hardened by plenty of exercise and a relatively uncomplicated existence, had recovered far more rapidly than it would have done from a similar wound a year ago. But he was a camp prisoner, for he had neither the stamina nor the nerve to try to get down the ladder.

He saw them coming along the shore, and waved and shouted excitedly—hurting himself in the process. Mary ran cautiously to greet them—for the child inside her was big enough to reduce her to a kind of sedate scamper. She and Barbara flung their arms round each other and, like a reflex action, immediately began laughing and crying. Avery was amused at the spectacle. Tom fumed impotently and impatiently from his perch on the rock.

Both Barbara and Avery were ravenously hungry. There was no meat in camp, but they took the edge off their hunger with fruit. Then, while Barbara finished telling their story, Avery went to gather some crabs—the most immediately convenient source of meat—for a main course. Presently, with the crab meat cooked and greedily devoured, they allowed themselves the luxury of whisky. There was not much whisky left, and Tom had disposed of another of the few remaining bottles for what he described apologetically as impurely medicinal purposes.

But Barbara did not need to use whisky to lean on any more. She had something stronger.

Mary seemed to sum it up rather neatly when, not entirely as a result of her second glass, she made an oddly formal toast. 'To the four of us—and to a kind of love that seems to split four ways.'

To Avery, it was a remarkably perceptive description. Obviously, in the deep sense, he could not love either Mary or Tom as he loved Barbara; but he loved them just as surely. They had become his friends and his family. They belonged to him. Without them, he felt, he could not be entirely human. He was even glad to acknowledge his dependence, and raised his glass in salute.

During the afternoon, Avery went on a brief hunting expedition to replenish the meat supply. Although he did not say anything about it to the others, and although he, too, was still elated at being able to bring Barbara back safely, he was convinced that the struggle with the golden people was by no means over. Certainly they had taken a beating, and one of their number was perhaps dead or seriously injured; but, from what he already knew of them, Avery was of the opinion that they would hardly care to let the situation stay as it was. They were a proud and arrogant people, glorying in their physical strength and contemptuous of what they regarded as lesser beings. The rescue must have hurt them spiritually as well as physically. They would not be content to let matters stand. For them, what had happened would be merely round two of the contest. Sooner or later, they would try for a conclusion. Above all, it would be necessary to their self-respect.

So thought Avery as he went to *their* colony of rabbitypes and indulged in what had become merely a routine execution. When he had acquired four of the small creatures, he made his way back to camp. He did not walk as he usually walked—with a jaunty self-assurance—he walked like a man who might be hunted, who might—at any moment—suddenly encounter his pursuers. He was afraid, and he knew there was reason to be afraid. Until peace could be established with the golden people, or until they could be decisively broken, the inhabitants of Camp Two would have to accustom themselves to living in a state of war. Twice Avery doubled back on his tracks and waited in ambush for any possible follower. But there was no one. Only his own fears.

That evening, after they had eaten and were luxuriating in the intimate companionship of the firelight, Tom brought up the subject of the golden people and their possible future actions.

'If you ask me, which you didn't,' he said laconically, after a brief silence, 'those javelin-happy bastards are going to try to give us a dose of massive retaliation. . . . I only hope they don't pull anything till I'm back on active service.'

'They've probably had enough to keep them quiet for a few days,' remarked Avery. But that was simply propaganda. He didn't really believe it. He only wanted to whistle to keep his—and everyone else's—spirits up.

'There's one consolation,' observed Mary.

'They'll have a hard job attacking us in camp.'

'I just hope they try,' said Barbara violently. 'Nothing would give me greater pleasure than to heave a few chunks of rock down on the heads of those—those pepped-up savages!'

Avery smiled. 'Let's hope the pleasure is deferred until—' he hesitated. He wanted to say 'until Tom is better, until you've both had your babies, and until we're all dying of old age.' Instead he went on: '—until we've all had a bit of a rest. . . . Personally, I'd be quite happy to call it quits—if they would.'

Tom snorted. 'They aren't the kind to settle for a drawn game.'

'No,' said Avery, suppressing a shiver. 'I don't suppose they are. . . . Well, it's about time for you and Mary to turn in. You both looked washed up. I'll take the first watch, then Barbara can do a spell.'

'We'll watch together,' said Barbara firmly.

Mary argued. 'You two have done all the work today. Tom and I are quite capable of—'

'That's an order,' smiled Avery. 'Am I or am I not the leader of the expedition?'

'No,' said Tom. 'You're just a boy scout with delusions of grandeur.' He turned to Mary. 'Come on, big tummy. If we don't do what the nasty man says, he'll never give us our good conduct medals.'

Despite her protests, Mary looked relieved when Tom took her into their tent.

Barbara's fears that her experiences of the previous day and night might cause her to lose the baby she had recently conceived were now quiescent. Her stomach was feeling perfectly normal once more and she began to feel that, barring any more drastic strains, she would carry the baby to full term.

She was glad that she had become pregnant. She knew now how badly she wanted to have Avery's child. And, too, because Mary was pregnant, she felt that it would somehow bring the four of them even closer together.

While she and Avery stayed on watch, they kept themselves awake by thinking of names. If the child was a boy, Avery wanted to call him Jason. Barbara objected that the other children (what other children?) would laugh at him. He must be called Andrew. But Avery had once taught an Andrew—a ghastly boy with a penknife and a penchant for using it on his friends—so Andrew was out. The game went on—a delightful, nonsensical game—it seemed for hours. They exhausted the possible boys names, and finally compromised on Dominic. Then they started on girls' names.

And then the tragedy happened.

There had been a few muffled noises from the tent where Tom and Mary were sleeping, but nothing out of the ordinary. Suddenly, however, they heard a deep groan—and were unable to tell whether it was Mary or Tom. Then the groan became a high, desolate cry; and they knew it was Mary.

Tom burst out of the tent. 'For Christ's sake!' he babbled. 'Something's happening! Something's happening to Mary.'

Something was indeed happening to Mary.

Barbara had been afraid of miscarriage. Mary had not. But the strain and anxieties of the last two days had placed too much of a burden on her. And her body was lightening the burden in the only way it knew how. Ironically, it was Mary who had to pay the price. . . .

They managed to get Tom away from her—Avery made him officially take over the watch—while they did what they could to help. It was precious little.

Neither Avery nor Barbara had ever been present at a birth before—to say nothing of a miscarriage—but fortunately Barbara had gained a little useful knowledge from her role as a nurse in that imaginary hospital projected regularly on ten million television screens in some far corner of the universe.

The contractions were quick and fierce. And so, mercifully, was the entire miscarriage. Within twenty minutes, Avery held in his bloodied hands the tiny, pathetic body of a five-months' old baby—curled up like a sad, miniature Buddha, its umbilical cord almost as thick as the perfectly formed arms and legs. Avery held the baby almost literally in the palm of his hand. In the other hand he held the placenta—still joined to it by a cord that was so recently a cord of life.

The baby was like a manikin, not dead but sleeping. There was the bleak illusion that suddenly, miraculously it would awake.

'Wrap it up!' commanded Barbara in a hard voice. 'Wrap it up and take it away.'

Mary was crying hysterically. Barbara tried to comfort her.

Avery found a piece of cloth. It was probably somebody's shirt or vest. He didn't know and he didn't care. He swathed the baby in it tenderly, as if he were afraid of disturbing it, as if at any moment it might cry. Then he went out of the tent.

He was going to leave the camp and take it away. But Tom wouldn't let him.

'I want to see my child.'

'Tom, it's—'

'I want to see my child.' Tom's voice had the same kind of hardness as Barbara's.

Avery carefully unwrapped the small bundle, and in the flickering firelight he and Tom gazed at the puckered but still strangely serene features.

'He would have been a nice little chap,' Tom managed to say. 'He was a he, wasn't he?'

'I—I'm sorry, Tom. I don't know.' Avery was himself wretched with Tom and Mary's sorrow. 'Do you want me to find out?'

'No,' said Tom in that hard voice. 'Don't disturb him. Let him rest now. He's had a rough time. . . . He deserves a bit of rest, doesn't he?'

Avery tried to stop the tears running down his face. He tried to will them back into his treacherous eyes. But they wouldn't go.

As they gazed at the quiet wreck of a child that was never to be, his tears and Tom's fell upon its small and oddly wise face. And mingled—a greeting and a benediction. A farewell. The first and the last that it would ever receive in the world of men.

'I'd better go to Mary,' said Tom at last. 'She'll need me now. She'll need me an awful lot.'

'Tom, I—' Avery didn't know what to say.

And oddly, it was Tom who comforted *him*. 'Richard,' he said quietly, 'you don't have to say anything. I know. He would have belonged to all of us. That's how it will always be now. Whatever happens belongs to all of us. . . . I'm going to stay with Mary. We'll be all right.' He turned towards the tent.

Avery covered the baby tenderly. It was still warm—warm with the cruel illusion of life.

TWENTY-FIVE

AVERY DID NOT BURY the baby until shortly before dawn. Barbara would not let him leave the camp in darkness, and so the fragment of wreckage that was Tom and Mary's child lay in state, mutely on the rocky ground under a brilliant canopy of stars.

For the remainder of the night, no one slept. Physically, Mary was in better condition than any of them had dared hope. But the grief had frozen in her. She became dry-eyed and empty. There was a stone in her heart, and nothing that Tom could do would prise it out. The stone would remain with her, not for always but until time itself had worn the edges off, leaving only a hard, small roundness. . . .

Avery left the camp at first light, taking with him a tomahawk and the now cold little bundle of colder hopes. He did not go very far from the camp. He went to the stream where they got their water, and then looked for a tall tree—one that would be easily identifiable. He found one almost at the water's edge. Idiotically, he thought to himself: 'Baby will like that—shade from the sun, and the sound of running water. . . . He shouldn't be too lonely here, because we shall be coming close to him every day.'

Then he laid the bundle down and began to hack a little grave out of the soft earth with his tomahawk.

At last it was deep enough. He laid the baby—still wrapped in one of Tom's shirts—in soil that was now warmer than its own body.

Avery was no great believer in God. But there were things he felt, things he had to say. Saying them was different than just thinking them—even if there was no one to hear. Speech itself was a kind of ceremony. It was all he had to offer by way of a requiem.

'Here,' he said, speaking in a firm but quiet voice, 'I commit a part of those I love and a part of Earth to the soil of a strange world. If this child had lived, he would have been a native of this world . . . . Perhaps the first member of an intelligent race ever to be born upon the planet. . . . But I don't know about that. There is so much I don't know. . . . I don't even know why we of Earth were brought here, or why God—if there is a god—denied this child the right to live. . . . But I do know that by this act of burial we establish a bond with this place that cannot be broken. We establish a bond and a kind of possession. For here is part of the substance of two human beings who have learned to share happiness and must now share sorrow. Their stillborn child, in the very nature of things, is now committed to enrich the life of a land in which we were once intruders. This is the ultimate intrusion, for we and the land now share something that is intimate and personal. . . . I cannot say any more, because I do not know if there is anything more to say. Except that . . . In the names of Tom and Mary, Barbara and me—Amen.'

Sad, and strangely puzzled by his own thoughts, Avery began to scrape the soil back into the hole. Then, when he had patted down the surface of the mound smoothly, he went back to camp.

As he walked, an absurd kind of mental arithmetic took possession of his mind. One, Tom is wounded; two, Barbara is abducted; three, indirectly a child is killed. One, two and three. What would four, five and six be? What would they all add up to in the end? One, Tom is wounded; two, Barbara is abducted; three, indirectly a child is killed. . . .

A child is killed. That was the important one. For now there was the promise of another child. And would that child, too, have to endure these unnecessary, other-than-normal hazards before and after birth? Must it learn to live with a fear it could not understand?

In the early morning, as he walked along the now well-known track, Avery found an answer to his question. . . .

Breakfast was a sullen, silent meal. Mary could walk, but she chose to stay in the tent, staring at nothing, wanting nothing, eating nothing. The others, however, were hungry. They resented the hunger and they resented the food; but they ate well, nevertheless. In some way—in the obscure chemistry of mind and body—grief had sharpened their appetites. They ate to distract themselves; but the distraction was not enough.

Avery gazed at Barbara as if she was a stranger. For a while he would have to make her into a stranger, because there was something to be done that he would have to do alone.

'Do you think you can pick up one of those

rocks, Tom?' he asked without preamble, indicating the permanent store of anti-siege ammunition that lay round the camp.

Tom raised an eyebrow. 'I can pick it up, and I can throw it as well. The shoulder that wasn't damaged is as good as ever.'

'Let's see you, then.'

Tom selected one of the rocks. 'What do you want me to do—try for a coconut?'

'Just throw it as far as you can.'

Because of the height of the camp above the rest of the shore, Tom managed to hurl the rock about thirty yards. But the effort made him wince.

However, Avery seemed satisfied. He turned to Barbara. 'Do you think you can do any better?'

'This isn't the time for games, Richard.'

'It isn't a game. Now have a shot.'

Barbara managed to beat Tom's effort by some ten yards.

'Not bad,' said Avery. 'If Camp Two was attacked, I should think the pair of you could keep them happy for quite a time—providing you didn't forget to dodge the javelins.'

'I'm not entirely eager to get myself punctured a second time,' observed Tom grimly. 'But we have the gun and we have you. So if they try to take us by storm—and what wouldn't I give to see them try!—it will just be like committing suicide the hard way.'

'You won't have the gun, and you won't have me,' retorted Avery. 'Not for a few hours, anyway. . . . I don't want to know whether you can conduct a massacre—just whether you can hold the fort.'

Tom understood. 'We can hold the fort, if we

have to. . . . But why don't you wait a few days, then—'

'Waiting doesn't seem to be such a good idea,' cut in Avery.

Barbara didn't want to understand. 'Richard, you are not going to go prancing off, today of all days. We have only just got back, and there's enough meat for the time being, and we can't let Mary feel—'

'Mary will be all right,' said Tom gently. 'Don't worry, Barbara. Richard hasn't done too badly by us so far. He knows what he's doing now.'

And then Barbara couldn't avoid understanding.

'Darling, you can't just—'

'Commit murder?' supplied Avery. 'I wouldn't have thought so, once. But I stopped being civilized the day before yesterday. All we wanted was to live in peace. As things stand, we can only live in fear. Unless we do something about it, what happened to Tom may happen to me—oh, yes, I'm scared for myself, all right—but even if nothing at all happens, and I wouldn't bet on it, there's still the fear. . . . You are carrying a baby. I don't want to risk any more variations on the theme of what happened to Mary.'

'Seconded and carried,' said Tom heavily. 'Incidentally, it has just occurred to me that they may have a little something similar to our pop-gun.'

'Good luck to them, then,' returned Avery grimly. 'I'm not a hero, and I don't much care for the medieval concept of chivalry. So I shan't be challenging anybody to a duel. . . . I expect that whoever dumped us in this place tried to make sure it was a pretty fair match. . . . But to hell with cricket! If I have to fight, then I'll damn well fight efficiently. No heroics—just plain, honest assassination, carried out as safely as possible.'

'My dear fellow,' said Tom with an attempt at lightness, 'it becomes increasingly clear that you would not have benefited by a public school education—I'm happy to say.'

'Darling,' said Barbara. 'Just come back, that's all. . . . Just come back.'

Avery kissed her briefly, almost impersonally. 'Look after Mary. And tell her that I've gone hunting. . . . ' He gave a bitter laugh. 'That's what it amounts to really, a glorified form of pest control.'

He took the loaded gun and an extra twelve rounds of ammunition. And he took a tomahawk and a knife. Barbara went with him as far as the trees; but he did not kiss her a second time. He merely held her for a moment. Already he had begun to hate himself, had begun to feel unclean because of the thoughts in his mind and the somehow grossly physical lust for vengeance.

He was actually eager to get at the golden people. The knowledge appalled him. As he walked, the gun in his pocket slapped against his leg rhythmically. It seemed to have a will of its own. At times, it seemed as if he was simply following the gun.

He knew now the direction to take, and he was in a hurry. He thought he would reach the enemy camp—how easy it was to think of them as enemies! — in less than a couple of hours.

But strange things began to happen. Things that did not augur well for the future. Twice he caught his foot in the exposed roots of trees, and fell down. Once he came across a small family of rhinotypes and had to make a wide detour. One rhinotype would have been no problem; but five invited respect.

Eventually, he struck the stream that supplied the golden people with water. Struck was an almost literal description, because he fell into it. He was walking too close to the edge, and the soft earth gave way, so that he fell spluttering into about five feet of water. As he got to his feet, he glimpsed a long shape on the opposite bank and heard a splash. He scrambled out quickly. The 'crocodile', floating in a kind of relaxed frustration, met his frightened gaze with an unwavering and baleful glare.

It was not until Avery had travelled another mile or so that he realized he had lost the gun. Letting out a string of profanities, he retraced his steps to the stream. The 'crocodile' was still in the water; but on the far bank—either he had not noticed it before or it had not been there before—was the part carcass of something unidentifiably animal.

He contented himself with searching along the water's edge for a few minutes, but he did not find the gun. Then he tried to get the 'crocodile' away by throwing things at it, but the creature was not discouraged and even seemed to think it was some kind of game.

Presently, he gave the task up.

The gun was gone. Now he had nothing but a tomahawk and a knife. The sensible thing to do would be to go back to Camp Two. Enough had happened to convince any reasonable person that the project was hardly likely to have a satisfactory end after such a disastrous beginning. But Avery was no longer a reasonable person. He was a man obsessed by the thought of killing.

He cursed the 'crocodile', he cursed the gun, he

cursed the golden people—and he went on. Half an hour later, he had reached their camp.

He approached it cautiously, and observed it from a discreet distance for what seemed like hours but was, in reality, doubtless only a few minutes. There was no sign of life—not even a fire. Ergo no one was at home.

Avery waited a little longer, just to make sure. At last he could control himself no more, and went marching in. The portable bridge lay conveniently across the moat and, filled with a sense of anti-climax, Avery walked boldly over it.

He saw the hut where he had flung his burning bundle. The doorway was charred, but otherwise its structure was sound. He looked around in bewilderment. Then suddenly he heard a noise, and knew that the place was not entirely deserted.

It came from the undamaged hut, and it was a long low moan. Avery tiptoed across to the side of the doorway, waited and listened. Presently, there was another moan. It was hard to tell whether it was made by a man or a woman.

Avery could not stand the suspense any longer. He began to think his mind was playing tricks. Suddenly, with tomahawk raised and knife in hand, he sprang through the doorway.

Then he froze, and his bloodlust died.

The woman who had saved his life, who had taken the javelin thrust that had been meant for him, was lying on a kind of bed. In her hand was a small, dark, dullish object shaped like an egg with a kind of handle. The small end of the egg was pointing at him. There seemed to be a shimmering at its centre. Perhaps it was an optical illusion.

Zleetri's abdomen was heavily bandaged, but the stain of her wound showed through.

She and Avery stared intently at each other for a moment or two, then another moan forced its way through her lips. She was no longer the powerful, independent golden woman. She was only a drab heap of flesh, shrunken by pain and loneliness and loss of blood. She was dying.

Avery knew nothing about her, except that she was dying. He remembered only why he had come here and was ashamed.

Slowly, he laid the tomahawk and the knife down. The egg-shaped mechanism in her hand followed his movements.

'Zleetri,' he said. 'I am so sorry.' He took a step towards her. The light at the end of the thing in her hand winked momentarily bright, and he felt a sharp burning on the skin of his stomach. But then the light faded, and the burning sensation with it. She laid the instrument down on her breast.

And she smiled at him.

He went to her side and knelt down.

'Ree-char,' she said. 'Ree-char.'

Avery took the thing from her weak fingers and put it to one side. He held her hand.

Oh, God! he thought. Why can't we talk to each other? Why can't I give her some comfort? Why can't I tell her even the inadequate things. There, but for her charity, lies Richard Avery. Oh, God! Why are there such barriers—such stupid, senseless barriers of language between us?

But there is no God, he thought angrily. There is no God—because a baby has died, because a woman is dying and because we who are left want to slaughter each other like animals. What has God to do with such predicaments? There is no other god but life. Life is the only holy thing. And when that goes that is the death of God.

She moaned again. 'Ree-char!' She gripped his hand tightly. Her voice wa beseeching. She could say nothing but his name, yet her eyes were eloquent.

Remembering the sign she had made, he touched his fingers to her forehead and to his. 'Dear Zleetri,' he murmured. 'Dear enemy, dear friend. Why—why in heaven's name couldn't we find out how to live with one another? But you aren't concerned with that any more, are you? . . . Did you know that even to us of a different race you and your kind are beautiful? We hated you, and yet we admired you. You, I think, despised us and perhaps you underestimated us. . . . But no more of that. I wish I could help you. You were such a proud and lovely being. . . . I wish I could help you. . . . '

'*Ree-char!*' The word was a scream, a tired scream torn from a tired body. She writhed in pain, yet was hardly strong enough to move her limbs.

'*Ree-char!*' She pointed to the thing he had taken from her.

He understood. He thought he understood, and put it back in her hand.

She tried to hold it, turning the small end towards her breast. She tried twice, and each time it dropped out of her shaking fingers. Then she pleaded for his help.

It was not in words—not even in a look. It was something fundamental, something so deep as to be able to bridge the chasm between race and race.

Avery nodded his comprehension, then kissed her lightly on the forehead. She managed to smile at him—there was even a flicker of pride in her face—and he knew that he had not offended.

He took the weapon—for such it surely was—

placed it carefully in her hand with her forefinger resting on a small stud, and then helped her to lift her arm so that the thing pointed to her breast.

'Zleetri,' he said. 'Sleep well, my dear one.'

She pressed the stud. There was a sudden shaft of light, a thin brief arrow of radiance. But no sound. And instantly a tiny hole had been burned into her body.

She gave a great sigh, as of utter contentment. Then her body sagged. Zleetri was dead.

Avery stared wonderingly at her for a few moments, as if he were in a trance. Then he came back to life, back to a harsh frame of reality. His mind began to operate again.

If Zleetri had been left alone, it was surely not because the rest had taken it into their heads to go hunting. They could hardly be as callous as that. And if they were not hunting, and if they were all absent—then, goddammit, they must have cooked up something really important. There was only one answer. He snatched up his weapon and turned to go.

He had already got out of the hut. Then suddenly he stopped and turned back. He went to Zleetri's body and took the weapon, putting it in his pocket. Then he laid her arms by her side and closed her eyes. He wanted to do something else—he desperately wanted to do something else for her. But there was nothing more. Nothing at all.

He went outside once more and tossed the weapon into the moat. Then he crossed the little bridge at a run.

Please, he gasped, as he sprinted through the trees and across patches of grassland, please let me get back in time!

He tried to imagine what would be happening at Camp Two. Then he tried not to imagine. What a bloody, cretinous oaf he had been to choose to make his reprisal raid today! Great, stupid, bloody-minded minds think alike, he told himself bitterly. He and the rest of the golden people must have passed very close to each other on their missions of vengeance.

As if to punish himself for his stupidity, he pushed his weary limbs to the limit of endurance. Literally to the limit. For it was not until he fell down, tried to get up, and fell down again, that he realized he would have to walk for a spell. In any case, he told himself bitterly, what good would he be if he got back to Camp Two a complete physical wreck.

But it was not long before he started to run once more. Eventually he had to ration himself to a hundred paces running and a hundred paces walking.

When he was still half a mile away from Camp Two, he noticed the plume of smoke above the tree tops. He had run himself into a state when he could not think clearly. He gave a last burst, and knew that he would have to walk the rest of the way. In any case, it would be a fine bloody thing—and about all he deserved—if he ran straight into the enemy. As his heart-beats slowed down a little and the non-thinking fog cleared out of his head, he began to wonder about the plume of smoke. It was a thick one—far too thick for an ordinary camp fire.

Sanity came back, and he kept to the trees as much as possible. He did not break out of cover until he was no more than about seventy yards from the rock.

He had already discovered what the plume of smoke was. By direct assault, Camp Two was pretty well impregnable. So the golden people, logically enough, were simultaneously attacking and trying to burn the occupants out. While two men kept the defenders busy by an exchange of rocks—they were obviously saving their javelins for the in-fighting stage—the remaining woman was bombarding them with fire arrows from a distance of perhaps fifty yards.

The entire scene was at the same time frightening, farcical, absurd and utterly deadly. It was a frolic and a nightmare. It was a glorious children's adventure. But the play was macabre and in earnest. There would be no cream cakes for tea after this escapade. Only death or injury for the vanquished.

The woman with the cross-bow and fire arrows was extremely methodical. She was less than twenty yards from Avery, and, fortunately her back was towards him. She had set up a little fire and was dipping the treated arrow-heads into its flames.

Beyond her, Avery could see that one of the tents at Camp Two had disappeared—into ashes, presumably—and the other was already burning. Mary—at least, it appeared to be Mary—was trying to beat the fire out while the other two kept the attackers at bay with their siege ammunition. One of the golden people kept trying to get in close to scale the rock while the other attempted to cover him. So far, apart from the destruction caused by the fire arrows, the attackers did not appear to be getting the best of the exchange. But perhaps the battle had not been going very long. Nevertheless, if Camp Two had been at ground level, doubtless it would all have been over by now.

Avery took a deep breath, willed some energy into his aching limbs, and sprinted towards the woman, tomahawk raised. He could so easily have killed her. Intent upon her task, she did not even hear him coming.

He could so easily have killed her. But even as the tomahawk was descending, the thought of Zleetri flashed through his mind. He saw again her once magnificent body. He saw it beaten and shrivelled by death.

He could not kill.

Instead he flung himself bodily upon the woman, knocking all the breath out of her with an anguished grunt. Then he smashed the flat of his hand hard into the back of her neck.

He snatched the cross-bow and tomahawked it into uselessness. He did not even turn to see how the woman was faring. She was coughing, retching and sobbing all at once. She would be out of action for quite a while.

He picked himself up, glanced at the rock, and saw Barbara and Tom dodging a rain of fairly small missiles and at the same time trying to stop one of the golden people from circling round to climb up behind them.

The sight acted as a booster to Avery's fatigue-heavy limbs. He lifted his tomahawk, gave a dreadful cry that was almost a snarl and rushed upon the nearest attacker.

The man turned in surprise. But he reacted almost instantly. He dropped the stones from his hands and picked up the two javelins that were lying at his feet.

Avery was fifteen yards away and closing the distance fast. As the first javelin came, he flung the tomahawk. The javelin missed. So did the tomahawk.

Avery still had his knife, and came on without pause. The second javelin was raised; and this time the look on his antagonists's face told Avery that he could not miss.

But, ridiculously, the look of triumph gave way to a look of total surprise. The man swayed uncertainly. The javelin fell from his hand even as Avery buried the blade of the hunting knife in hard golden flesh just below the rib cage.

The man fell forward, almost taking Avery with him. It was only then that he saw the other tomahawk—Tom's favourite—with its cutting edge buried deep between the shoulder blades.

Avery stared round him in a daze. Everything seemed to have stopped. The whole scene appeared frozen as in a photograph. A few yards down the shore, the woman had managed to get herself up into a half-sitting position. Barbara stood poised on the rock with a tent pole in her hand. Tom was huddled up like a bundle of old clothes at the base of the rock. Mary was leaning over to look down at Tom. The other golden man had retreated a few paces. There was a blank look on his face. Clearly, he found it hard to believe what he saw.

Then the scene snapped back into movement. The remaining attacker backed warily away, back towards the woman—whose moans became drowned in Mary's sudden scream and Tom's volley of groaning obscenities. Barbara held grimly on to the tent pole, and the man at Avery's feet was the only motionless person, for death had been no less swift than surprising.

Avery went towards Tom. But Tom, despite a

ten-foot drop and the wound in his shoulder, was already picking himself up.

'Did you see that shot?' he gasped.

'For Christ's sake! Are you hurt?'

'Balls to that! Of course I'm hurt. I've still got a hole in my shoulder you could stick a cigar in. Let's cry about it later. . . . Did you see the shot, Richard? I got the bastard plumb centre—threw myself overboard in the process, but it was worth it.'

He tried to put his weight on his left leg, and sat down suddenly with a yelp.

'Now I've buggered myself at the other end, too. . . . Look at them, Richard. Look at the master race.'

Mary and Barbara were both calling down to them, talking together. But Tom didn't seem to hear.

Avery followed his gaze along the shore. The golden people, the only two that were left now, were in full retreat. The man was half supporting the woman. They were limping along as fast as they could, expecting to be pursued, and hoping that they could reach the relative security of the trees.

Avery sighed. 'Do you think I ought to—'

'No,' said Tom, magnanimous in victory. 'Let the poor devils go. They've got problems. . . . Somehow I don't think they'll be coming back. They've had too much pride knocked out of them. . . . You know, Richard,' he moved his leg and winced. 'It's beginning to look like game, set and match.'

TWENTY-SIX

THERE WAS NOTHING but darkness.

There was nothing but darkness and the awful, infinite splendour of stars.

He came to a sun; and the sun had given birth to planets. One of the planets was blue and white with clouds, green with oceans, red and yellow with islands.

'This,' said the voice, 'is home. This is the garden. This is the world where you will live and grow and understand. This is where you will discover enough but not too much. This is where life is. It is yours.'

The voice was gentle, but it came echoing down a draughty tunnel of centuries. Its sound was thunder; and the thunder shook his sleeping mind.

Christine swam towards him through the stars. And the stars became the leaves of an English autumn, brown and gold.

Christine whispered: 'Wherever you are, whatever you do, my dear one, I am part of it. You have made of our love something new. You have made it bright. You have given it freedom. . . . She, now, is the one. So hold her, and hold us both. . . . '

He wanted to speak, but there were no words. Christine, remote and beautiful, dissolved in the steep canyons of darkness, gently like a snowflake, like a dying point of light. . . .

Avery stirred, opened his eyes, gazed in the half light at Barbara sleeping tranquilly by his side.

Dear Barbara, he thought, warm and wonderful Barbara. Not Christine. Not greater than Christine, not lesser. Strangely not even other than Christine. Simply the one to hold. A woman and Woman. . . .

He touched her face. He felt the contours and marvelled at the living flesh. He knew that he would always want to look at her like this, as if for the first time.

Then he remembered the golden people and Zleetri. He remembered the battle and the dead man whom he finally had to carry away for burial . . . . He and Barbara were enriched somehow by the memory of shared dangers—and of a private sadness that could never wholly be shared.

He sat up carefully, not wishing to disturb her. She needed to rest, for there had been much to endure—there still would be much to endure—and inside her there was a tiny cellular miracle, quietly growing like a hidden fruit.

He sat up, sniffed the air luxuriously and gazed through the doorway of the tent at the briefly mysterious world of pre-dawn. There were hardly any signs now of yesterday's battle. The wreckage of the old tents—and one of the trunks that had been badly burned—had already been cleared away. It was almost as if the conflict might never have been . . . .He got out of bed and stretched himself. Then he dressed and went outside.

The camp was what it always was—a small, known, untidy, familiar place of refuge. A home and a sanctuary. A magic circle, redolent of cooking and companionship, of living and loving.

No one else was about, and Avery moved quietly. Tom and Mary had had the hardest time of all. He hoped they would be able to rest now. They needed to rest for quite a while.

Avery stood on the small rock that was Camp Two and gazed at his private kingdom, the island and the sea. A red sun was beginning to climb over the edge of the world. The sky was still and clear. It was going to be a fine day. . . . Another day to fill with the incomprehensible privilege of being alive. . . .

The sea was flat and softly silvered by the growing light. He gazed idly towards the water's edge. Then rubbed his eyes and looked again.

It was there.

It was still there.

On the shore, not far from the water line, not far from the rock, stood a small pedestal. It supported a machine that looked something like a compact and incredibly neat typewriter. The paper was already fed into it from an endless roll.

Avery had seen such a machine before. In another time and place. In a dream: In a situation that was of a greater stature than dreams, yet dictated by the same unreasonable logic, and with the same vivid compulsions.

A great bubble of excitement grew inside him. A bubble of excitement and tension. He scrambled down the ladder. As he did so, the typewriter that was not a typewriter began to print out its message.

Do not be alarmed, it said. *The experiment has reached a satisfactory conclusion. It would be of value, however, to have the observations of the subjects.*

Avery relaxed a little. The machine had lost none of its inscrutability. He was surprised to find suddenly that he was filled not with resentment—not even with fear—but with amusement.

He put his hand towards the keys. *This subject,* he tapped out, *is nonplussed.*

The machine retaliated. *Please amplify.*

Nonplussed, responded Avery, *means perplexed, bewildered, mystified. . . . The subject has all that and heaven, too.*

Please clarify.

Why should I? You hardly set a good example yourself. . . .

Please clarify. It is important.

Avery was beginning to enjoy himself. *Only living is important,* he tapped out. *That is the conclusion the subject has drawn as a result of the experiment.*

There was a pause. Then the machine continued. *Are you happy?*

Yes.

Are you healthy?

Yes.

Do you regret the experiment?

It was Avery's turn to pause. Finally, he typed *No.*

Do you wish now to return to your natural habitat?

Suddenly Avery thought about the others. He turned towards the rock. Barbara was already up. She had just at that moment come out of the tent, and stood staring at him incredulously.

'Sweetheart, get the others,' he called. Uncle has suddenly come to life again. He wants to know how we're all getting along. . . . And, Barbara, he wants to know if we'd like to go home.'

Barbara recovered herself remarkably quickly. 'I'll get Tom and Mary,' she shouted. 'Tell Uncle not to disappear for a while. There are a few things I'd like to say to that little joker.'

Avery tapped out: *Hold your horses. Everybody wants to exercise their democratic rights.*

Query: Which horses? Which democratic rights?

Avery was delighted by 'Uncle's' evident confusion. *The ones you might ride away on, and free speech for all.*

Barbara was first down the ladder. She held it at the bottom while Mary helped Tom on to the top rung. Despite his heavy fall of the previous day, and apart from the fact that the wound in his back had bled a little, he was really recovering far better than anyone had expected. So was Mary. She still looked pale and tired, but that was all.

Tom came gingerly down the ladder and reached the bottom without mishap. Mary followed him.

With Barbara, they joined Avery and stood in front of the machine, marvelling.

'We could always crown it with a large boulder,' suggested Tom at length.

Avery grinned. 'An excellent idea—provided you don't ever want to go back to Earth.'

'What!'

'It just asked me whether we'd like to return — quote — to our natural habitat.'

'Natural habitat!' snorted Tom. 'I'd just like to be in the natural habitat of the character at the other end of this little gadget.'

The machine came to life again. *Since the experiment has been concluded successfully, the question of the rehabilitation of all participants now arises.*

'Let me get at it!' exploded Barbara. She began to hit the keys savagely. *You mean the rehabilitation of all survivors, Uncle. What about the golden people that were killed? What about the baby that died? Rehabilitate them if you can.*

Casualties are greatly regretted, came the answer. *But in an experiment of this nature, some hazard must be accepted. Perhaps there is justification in the fact that the issue involved is great.*

What was the nature of the experiment? tapped Avery.

The response came immediately: *Culture dynamics.*

Mary looked at the printed roll. 'Ask him,' she said, with a touch of bitterness, 'what the marvellous issue was. . . . I don't suppose that will make any sense either.'

Avery tapped out of the message, and again the answer came as soon as he had finished.

The issue involved is the ultimate domination of the second stellar rim sector in the second linear quadrant of the galaxy.

'Shit and derision!' snapped Tom. 'This thing is taking the mickey out of us with a load of gobbledygook. Here, let me have a go.'

He tapped out: *Now cut the crap and get down to something a man can understand. How the hell did you get us here? Where are we, anyway? What's it all about? And finally, if you've got enough bloody decency–which I doubt–to be intelligible, what do you propose to do about repatriation?*

'There,' he said, when he'd finished. 'That ought to silence the bastard.'

But it didn't. The machine began to click busily.

In the order of the questions given, the answers are as follows, it printed.

At the collection area, each of you discovered a crystal which produced the apparent effect of unconsciousness. In fact, you were not rendered unconscious in the sense of being immobile and helpless. However, the effect of the crystal was to anaesthetize your memory, while at the same time allowing remote control to be exercised over your actions. This, of course, involved a temporary suspension of freedom of thought, which was unavoidable. Each of you, operating under control, picked the crystal up and retained it. To accommodate you by explaining the matter in crudely simple terms, it is possible to say that each crystal acted as a kind of psychic radio which allowed the transmission of direct instructions to you. You, yourselves, apparently operating as free agents, obtained the equipment for the journey. As instructed, you then travelled to a rendezvous where it was convenient for you to be taken aboard a transport vessel at a time when it was unlikely that the operation would be observed by others of your species. In fact, the rendezvous took place within forty terrestrial hours of control being established.

'Stop me!' said Tom helplessly. Seeing the look on his face, Avery wanted to laugh, but he was afraid that the laughter might become hysterical.

The machine continued.

Your present location is an island on the fourth planet of the star known to terrestrial observers as Achernar. It is about seventy terrestrial light-years from your own sun.

After a momentary pause, the machine went on once more.

In that section of the galaxy which can only be described to you as the rim sector of the second linear quadrant, there are two intelligent races at present on the threshold of space flight. To one of them must fall the ultimate responsibility for control of that area. Your own race and that of what you call the golden people are the two concerned. It was the object of the experiment–by assembling representative components of each culture pattern in a neutral background and under conditions of stress–to determine which of the races possessed the most useful psychological characteristics. This has now been established. Certain techniques–analagous to your system of radar, telephotography and parabolic sound detectors–have made it possible for you, the subjects, to remain under careful observation. The results of the experiment are conclusive.

'This,' said Mary quietly, 'beats the band.' She looked at her companions helplessly.

The machine went on.

All surviving subjects of the experiment are given the choice of returning to their planet of origin, or remaining on Achernar Four. This planet does not possess an indigenous race of intelligent beings. It is therefore available for development. However, any subject who wishes to return to his or her planet of origin can be so transported at speed. For various reasons, one of which is the mental health of the subject, it will be necessary to implant an amnesia block in those who wish to return. Remembering nothing of the experiment, they will not be subject to retroactive emotional stress. On return financial compensation and temporary therapeutic care can be arranged. Your decisions are awaited.

There was silence.

Avery and Barbara, Tom and Mary looked at each other. Bewilderment was on every face. Bewilderment and tension.

It was possible to go back to Earth! The knowledge hammered like an incessant drumbeat in Avery's brain. He thought about London. For so long it had been vague and cloudy; but the possibility of return somehow brought the city into sharp focus, presented it to his inward eye as a series of magic lantern slides. . . . Kensington Gardens, Piccadilly Circus, theatres, shops, people, the Underground, Big Ben, the Embankment, the Bayswater Road. . . .

He saw them all. He could hear the traffic, the street musicians, the starlings in Whitehall and Trafalgar Square. Big Ben struck; and he could smell the scent of roasting chestnuts, of crowded restaurants, of late roses in a flower seller's basket.

He could see and smell—he could almost touch. And suddenly he felt a shock that seemed physical in its impact. He didn't want London. He knew he didn't want any of it. For London meant forgetting. London meant the loss of what had grown between him and Barbara. . . . And Tom. . . . And Mary. . . . London meant gaining so little, and losing so much.

He looked at the others and knew that they, too, did not want to surrender the memories of all that had happened to bind them close. On Earth they had all been lonely people. Here, seventy light-years from Piccadilly Circus, they were no longer alone.

But there was another reason for not going back—a reason that was as yet only half-formed in their minds. Here, there was a chance to create. A chance to start from nothing, with only their hands and their hopes. A chance to make something new. . . . A hell of a chance! But one, thought Avery, that was worth taking.

Unconsciously, he put his arm round Barbara's shoulder. They looked at each other—as Tom and Mary were looking at each other. They looked at each other and understood.

'Shall I give Uncle his answer?' asked Avery quietly.

Barbara shook her head, and stepped up to the machine. 'There's something else,' she said. 'We have a right to know.'

She tapped the message out. *We want to see you. You have done a great deal to us without our consent. We have a right to see you.*

The answer was enigmatic. *It will not be of value. There is no acceptable true image.*

Barbara persisted. *Nevertheless, we want to see you. Or are you afraid to be seen?*

There was a long pause. Then the machine printed out: *There is no true image. But judge for yourselves. The request is granted.*

Suddenly, there was a humming in the air. A humming as of all the bees in the universe concentrated into an invisible point, into a searing needle of sound.

Then the humming was cut off abruptly. And, farther along the shore, a great monstrous, blinding, golden ball—perhaps thirty yards in diameter—hovered just above the surface of the sand.

There was a tiny, dry crackle—Avery remembered it well—as of fine splinters of glass being broken. For a fraction of a second, the ball shimmered, then it disappeared.

Four people stood where it had been.

Two men and two women.

Four golden people.

One of them was Zleetri.

Avery took a step forward. But in the space of that single step, his desire to move was frozen.

The golden people were no longer golden people. They had changed into another Tom, another Mary, another Barbara—another Avery. Every detail was correct, even to Tom's bandage showing through the top of his shirt. Even to the burn mark—a scar of battle—on Mary's arm.

The other Avery spoke. 'Forgive our tricks. Do not be afraid. They were to show you that there is no true image. . . . Think of it as a technique similar to, but far more complex than, the protective coloration of the chameleon.'

Avery heard his own voice used by a mirror-image. But though he was numb with shock, his mind continued to work. . . . The voice, he was surprised to find, had not been stolen in a literal sense; for suddenly, and in great amazement, he heard himself speak.

'The tricks are not good enough. Show us, then, what is most nearly the true image.'

'As you wish,' said the other Avery.

The figures changed.

They changed into something that was familiar, yet inexplicable. They changed into monsters that were not monstrous, into people who were neither men nor women.

They changed into small, naked, brown-skinned, humanoid hermaphrodites. Hermaphrodites who also seemed like super quadruplets. For, in every detail, they were absolutely identical.

One of them spoke. It was not a man's voice, nor

was it a woman's voice. Nor yet was the sound displeasing.

'To you of Achernar, late of the Earth, from the controllers of the second linear quadrant, greetings. For what has happened, we do not ask your forgiveness. We ask only your understanding; since your race is destined to become our inheritors.

'It will be hard for you to understand. Our science and our culture are more than a million earth-years ahead of yours. Long ago we developed the technology to take us into space; and in becoming space-borne, we acquired the attitudes and the responsibilities that become the burden of all space-oriented forms of intelligent life. We have no planetary home. It is lost in time. Nor do we now need one. For long ago our techniques enabled us to become immortal. And because of this we are dying. That is why we set ourselves the task of discovering our true inheritors. It is to them that we must ultimately entrust the future of intelligent life in the second quadrant.'

Avery found his tongue again. 'If you are immortal, then you cannot die.'

The hermaphrodite smiled. 'Immortality was attained at the expense of fertility. We do not die of age. But no one can be immune to the laws of chance. Accident is our unvanquishable enemy. Few of us die by accident, yet fewer of us are born. In three or four millennia, we shall be extinct. Because of this we conducted the experiment. As a result, we shall ensure that in this sector one race only will eventually tap the secrets of the stars. The only other intelligent race—those whom you call the golden people, the inhabitants of the fifth planet of Alpha Centauri—will be inhibited. The people of your Earth are our inheritors.

'Your race will become our inheritors not because of your superior strength, for your strength is not superior; and not because of your superior intelligence, for there is little to choose. But of the forty groups placed on twenty islands of this planet, thirteen Earth-groups survived creatively, six Centaurian groups survived creatively and the rest disintegrated in conflict. The groups that survived did so not because they were strong—though strength was needed—but because they found another collective strength, which you inadequately call compassion....

'Of the thirteen surviving Earth groups, nine—including this one, for we see that your decision has been taken—have elected to stay here on Achernar. Of the six surviving Centaurian groups, none have elected to stay. . . .

'Compassion and the desire to create. In the end, they are the only qualities you will need. Perhaps one day you or the others of your kind will cross the seas of Achernar to unite. They are of different ethnic groups. Perhaps, in the end, you will develop a multi-ethnic culture. That, too, might be an experiment of some interest. . . .

'But now we leave you with the gift of a planet. Make of it what you will. It may be that, in the space of a generation or two, we shall return to observe your progress. Meanwhile, farewell.'

The four identical hermaphrodites simultaneously raised their left arms in a gesture that seemed vaguely similar to the ancient Roman salute.

'Wait!' said Avery desperately. 'There is so much we want to know. So much we don't understand.'

The hermaphrodite who had already spoken spoke once more. There seemed to be a hint of laughter in the voice.

'This is home. This is the garden. This is the world where you will live and grow and understand. This is where you will discover enough but not too much. This is where life is. It is yours.'

Then there was that penetrating sound as of a myriad bees. The humming stopped. Instantly it was as if the four beings had been obliterated by a ball of fire.

The sphere shimmered. Slowly it seemed to roll, liquid and blinding, towards Avery and Barbara and Tom and Mary.

They backed away.

It passed over the typewriter that was not a typewriter. And where it had passed there was nothing.

There came that other sound—the fine splintering of splintered glass. And suddenly, there was only sea and sky and land.

And four people, like sleep-walkers, like children waking and not yet quite awake.

Tom let out a great sigh and wiped the sweat from his forehead. 'Jesus!' he murmured. 'Jesus H! As far as I'm concerned seeing isn't believing any more. What do you make of it? What *can* you make of it?'

'It doesn't matter,' said Mary surprisingly. 'I mean *They* don't matter. They can talk about immortality and destiny and quadrants till they're blue in the face. That doesn't mean anything. Not to me. . . . What matters is that we have each other. It's enough.'

'Yes,' agreed Barbara, taking Avery's hand. 'It's quite enough. I don't know what they're up to—I don't even want to know. But they've given us a chance to find each other and ourselves. That satisfies me.'

Avery smiled. 'It doesn't satisfy me.'

But Barbara's brief disappointment vanished as he went on.

'Finding each other is the big thing, but it's only the first thing. Now we have to build. Not just a house or even—if we get enough children—a village. Not just comfort on a cosy little island for four. But some damn silly compulsive abstraction called civilization. . . . To hell with *Them!* We'll try to sort out a few of their riddles when we have nothing better to do in the evenings. But if it's true what *They* said, then sooner or later we're going to have to try our hands at boats. Then we can link up and really grow.'

'Pooh,' said Barbara. 'Let's wait till somebody comes to visit us.'

Avery ruffled her hair affectionately. 'Suppose they all think that? Come on, we can argue it out over breakfast. And then we must really look for a select plot of land for a house—the first house.'

As they went back to Camp Two, Avery began to think about *Them*. Despite the grotesque appearance, there had been something oddly familiar about them.

And suddenly he knew what it was.

He had seen that face—the four faces in one—and that smile before.

He had seen them seventy light-years ago in an

illustration in a geography book in an English schoolroom.

The smile on the face of the Sphinx. . . .

Filled with wonder, confusion—and a strange feeling of exhiliration—he helped Barbara to get fruit and some fresh water for breakfast.

The sun was still low, but there was every sign that it was going to be a hot day.

Perhaps, instead of looking for a piece of land to build on, he would paint.

Perhaps, while he was painting, he would dream of building a boat. . . .